It Was Too Intense
For A First Kiss.

There was no exploration, no tentative questioning. It was rich with mature desire, hard with the demand for recognition, seductive with the technique of a practiced lover. Both frightening and tantalizing, it held a promise of danger and a hint of ecstasy. No first kiss should be so bold.

Then Ann remembered. It wasn't a first kiss at all.

Cam drew back, looking down into her face. "I haven't forgotten when we did this before, Ann," he said huskily, running a finger down her cheek. "I don't believe you have, either."

Dear Reader,

Welcome to Silhouette Desire! Naturally, I think you've made a spectacular choice because, for me, each and every Silhouette Desire novel is a delightful, romantic, unique book. And once you start reading your selection I *know* you'll agree!

Silhouette Desire is thrilling romance. Here you'll encounter the joys and even some of the tribulations of falling in love. You'll meet characters you'll get to know and like...and heroes you'll get to know and *love*. Sensuous, moving, compelling, these are all words you can use to describe Silhouette Desire. But remember, words are not enough—you must *read* and get the total experience!

And there is something wonderful in store for you this month: *Outlaw*, the first in Elizabeth Lowell's WESTERN LOVERS series. It tells the story of rough-and-tough Tennessee Blackthorne...a man of fiery passions and deep emotions.

Of course, *all* of February's Silhouette Desire books are terrific—don't miss a single one! Until next month...

All the best,

Lucia Macro
Senior Editor

RAYE MORGAN

IN A MARRYING MOOD

SILHOUETTE *Desire*

Published by Silhouette Books New York

America's Publisher of Contemporary Romance

SILHOUETTE BOOKS
300 East 42nd St., New York, N.Y. 10017

IN A MARRYING MOOD

ISBN: 0-373-05623-0

First Silhouette Books printing February 1991

Books by Raye Morgan

Silhouette Romance

Roses Never Fade #427

Silhouette Desire

Embers of the Sun #52
Summer Wind #101
Crystal Blue Horizon #141
A Lucky Streak #393
Husband for Hire #434
Too Many Babies #543
Ladies' Man #562
In a Marrying Mood #623

RAYE MORGAN

favors settings in the West, which is where she has spent most of her life. She admits to a penchant for Western heroes, believing that whether he's a rugged outdoorsman or a smooth city sophisticate, he tends to have a streak of wildness that the romantic heroine can't resist taming. Raye's been married to one of those Western men for twenty years and is busy raising four more in her Southern California home.

One

Cam Sterling drove too fast.

Everyone in Crystal County knew it. Cam knew it himself, but that didn't stop him. There was an impatient restlessness in him that came to the surface when he got behind the wheel of one of those fast little sports cars.

You'll kill yourself one of these days!

How often had he heard that? Practically every day of his life since he'd turned sixteen and gone down to the DMV to get his license. Nineteen years of dire warnings, but he was still here.

He gunned the engine as he came to the hill off the state highway, anticipating the straightaway over the crest, even though it must have been five years since he'd been on this road. He'd driven it so often as a teenager, every nuance was engraved on his mind, and

the new potholes that had developed in the meantime
hardly mattered. Every time he came back to the valley for a visit home, it was as though he'd never left.
All the years of sitting in the back seat of a limousine
cruising the streets of New York City hadn't dulled the
thrill. This was the way a car ought to feel. This was
the way a man ought to drive.

There was no one in sight and he floored it, barely
watching as the indicator swung toward three digits.
He felt the wind whipping at his face, the power of the
roaring car as it gathered momentum, the sense of
flying, catapulting toward infinity.

This time he would do it. He had the car. He had the
skill. And he now had the confidence to go through
with it. He would take Outlaw's Pass at top speed.
That old bugaboo had taunted him for the last time....

He hardly had to touch the steering wheel. The car
obeyed his direction instantly, as though it could read
his mind. The car's wheels skidded, trying to hold the
road, trying to make the turn. For one heart-stopping
moment, he thought he'd lost it. But then the wheels
grabbed again and he was around the curve. He'd
made it. Triumph coursed through him and he let out
a rebel yell. It was an omen. He'd defeated the curve.

The sound, when it came, was loud, as though
someone had popped a balloon right next to his ear.
He knew it was a blowout before he had a chance to
react. And then there was gravel spitting and the car
was sailing into the brush along the side of the road.
He'd made it around Outlaw's Pass, but plain old bad
luck got him anyway.

* * *

Ann's headlights were on high beam; otherwise she probably wouldn't have caught sight of the car off the road just past Outlaw's Pass. But she did see it and she jerked the wheel on her little van, pulling over to the shoulder and jumping out to see if anyone was hurt.

The car was some sort of low, slinky foreign sports car she didn't recognize. It had hit an ironwood tree and though the fender was only slightly crumpled, smoke was coming out from under the hood. Ann steeled herself for what she might be dealing with here, pushing back emotion to leave her free to do what was necessary to help the situation. If someone were trapped inside . . .

Ignoring the smoke and the danger it might be signaling, she ran up to the car and fumbled with the latch on the door, noting at the same time that there was a man in the driver's seat, leaning over the steering wheel. She yanked open the door and grabbed him by the shoulders. He was alive, but he was groggy.

She hesitated a moment. Maybe he shouldn't be moved. But the smoke looked ominous. Better to risk it. Slipping down her hands, she hooked her arms under his shoulders and began to pull with all her might.

He was heavy, his body as hard as a rock under the silk suit. She was panting by the time she'd pulled him free of the car, and gasping for breath by the time she'd dragged him far enough away to feel safe. Actually, he had helped her. If he hadn't, she probably wouldn't have been able to get him out the way she had.

After stretching him out on a bed of leaves and twigs, she sat back to look at him, afraid of what she might see. He seemed to be stunned but not completely unconscious. He groaned, and she nodded, then looked back toward her van, debating whether to check him out further or make a dash for a phone to call the paramedics.

He moved, clearing his throat, and she looked down at him, for the first time really taking in his face. The breath stopped in her chest as she did so. His eyes were wide open. He was looking right at her and he was focusing just fine, but she hardly noticed. Her heart was beating very fast, and she was filled with wonder. She knew this man.

"Cam Sterling," she whispered. "Oh my God!"

The blue eyes closed for a moment and his handsome face grimaced in pain. He muttered an oath, and then the eyes focused on where she sat back, still staring at him as though mesmerized.

"Wow. That one got me for a minute," he muttered, wincing, then starting to pull himself up.

"No, wait! Lie back," she ordered, moving forward quickly and putting out a hand to force him to stay flat. "You've been in a car accident. You'd better stay still until we know what's been injured."

He looked at her, bemused, as though not quite sure why she should be giving him orders. "I'm going to be stiff tomorrow," he predicted. "I'm going to feel as though I've been put through a meat grinder." He sighed and shook himself.

Ann watched him, partly because of who he was, partly to make sure he wasn't hurt worse than was immediately apparent. He had been knocked silly, but that seemed to be all. He didn't look weak or vulnerable in any way. There was something vital about the man that seemed to overpower this little setback. He was resting, that was all, gathering strength to get back to normal.

When he spoke again, his words only confirmed her diagnosis. "I'll tell you what's been injured," he said, his voice stronger this time. He was gazing at her with rueful irony. "My pride, that's what. I still can't make Outlaw's Pass at top speed without something going wrong."

Exasperation spilled through her. He was still the same, still going for the rush that risk-taking gave him, still looking for fun above all else. Was this man ever going to grow up?

And yet, that boyish quality was a large part of his attraction.

"Is that what you were trying to do?" she demanded, torn between indignation and memories. He could have been killed! "Then you deserve this."

He didn't argue. "Of course I deserve it," he said pleasantly, his voice only slightly gravelly. "It's a small price to pay, though, for a chance at greatness."

"Greatness?" Men—what made them so irrational? She wanted to throttle him, only fate had already done that for her. And she wanted to comfort him, only she didn't dare. She'd never known a man in the last twenty years who could call up such conflicting emotions in her.

"You call taking Outlaw's Pass at top speed 'greatness'?" She clenched her hands into fists in frustration. "How can you say such a thing? Even if you had made it, no one would ever know but you. How can that be greatness?"

He was grinning at her with that slow, lazy, knowing grin that had turned her knees to water from the time she'd first seen him. The man had almost died, and the grin still worked.

"'Greatness' is a state of mind," he drawled. "It's all in how you see yourself."

She bit back the reply that first came to her. How could she be angry at a man whose eyes sparkled with humor like that, just after being smashed up in a car wreck?

He hadn't changed. His presence had always been magic. Even now she felt the pull of his compelling personality, the charisma that had captivated the entire female population of Covington High School the year Cam Sterling had come to study there. Every girl in town had dreamed of what life would be like married to a man like Cam. And when he'd flown off to college in the East without having made a choice among them, every girl had heaved a sigh of regret.

Had he ever found his own dream girl? Ann found herself glancing at his hand to look for evidence of a wedding ring, and hated herself for doing it.

"They say you shouldn't move an accident victim until he's received medical attention," she began, but she was too late. He was already pulling himself up and there was nothing she could do to stop him.

"I'm okay," he insisted. "Just a bit of a headache." He shook out each limb and did a deep knee bend before taking out a handkerchief and dabbing at a scratch on his hand. "No broken bones. No internal injuries. Just a little seepage. But there's plenty more where this red stuff came from."

"You don't know that for sure. I'll drive you to the emergency room at the hospital."

He seemed to tower over her, larger, thicker than she remembered him.

"I don't want to go to the hospital." He grimaced and glanced around. "What I am going to need is a ride to somewhere with a phone. Do you think you could provide me with that?" He looked toward her little van.

"Of course."

He looked at her, his eyes huge and sparkling. "I hope I'm not ruining your evening plans, Miss... What is your name?"

She'd been fully aware that he didn't recognize her from the beginning; still, it cut a bit to have it confirmed so clearly. There was no reason he should remember. She'd never been anything to him. She'd been going steady with one of his best friends, that was all. High school days—so long ago.

"Ann," she said crisply, not even contemplating adding the last name. If she said "Ann Dupree," would he connect her with Johnny? Or were those days so long gone that he didn't even remember the boy who'd considered him the best friend he ever had?

"Hello, Ann," he was saying, putting out his hand. "I'm Cam Sterling."

She shook hands gingerly, not wanting to give up anything to him just yet. "I know who you are. In fact, I was on my way out to the Sterling estate when I found you."

"You were?" He didn't seem to find that remarkable. "Great. Then you can give me a ride."

"Sure. After we visit the hospital."

He put a hand on her arm, his face completely serious. "I'm fine. I don't need to go to the hospital."

She pulled away from his touch, not because it was too familiar, but because it was too disturbing. She'd spent too many wasted years mooning over this man. She was never going to be that stupid again. "You were practically unconscious...."

His grin was back and he shrugged. "I was merely resting."

Her frustration level was being tried. She threw out her hands, palms up, beseechingly. "You need to be looked at by a trained professional."

He considered for a moment. From the gleam in his eyes, she could tell he was enjoying her concern, which made her want to whack him.

"All right," he conceded at last. "I'll call my mother's family physician to come out to the house to take a look. Okay? Does that mollify your nurturing instincts?"

She sighed, shoulders sagging in resignation. "All right. All right, let's go." She glanced toward the mangled car, which was no longer smoking.

He turned, following her gaze, and winced when he saw the damage. "Poor thing. I rented it in L.A. It seems a shame to do that to such a lovely piece of work. But I'm sure the rental company will accept a fat check to cover the repairs. I'll send someone out from my mother's to pick up the pieces."

She met his gaze and knew he read in her eyes what she was thinking—that the "pieces" could so easily have been his. He looked slightly bemused, as though he couldn't imagine why she should care one way or the other.

And neither could she, darn it! After all, this was Cam Sterling—the man who had disappointed Johnny. There was no reason at all to give him special consideration. She turned and led the way to her van.

"Creative Catering," he said, reading the name on the side panel as he came up behind her. "Is that you?"

"That's me." She unlocked the passenger door for him and started around to the other side. "And that was why I was on my way to your mother's place. She's considering using me for a series of parties she wants to throw this summer."

"The parties. Yes." He made a show of shuddering. "Don't remind me."

Ann got into the driver's seat and started the engine, but suddenly his hand was on the steering wheel.

"Do me one more favor, Ms. Caterer," he said pleasantly in the tone of one used to having others drop everything in order to do things that would make him happy. "I'm not ready to face my mother just yet. And though I don't much relish the thought of a hospital waiting room, I would like to stop somewhere for a cup of coffee or a cold drink." He smiled at her. "And we could get better acquainted."

She shook her head in exasperation. "Cam, really..." she began, then paled when she realized how easily she'd slipped into talking to him as she might have twenty years before.

But he didn't seem to notice. "Come on," he coaxed, his smile completely irresistible. "Indulge me. I've just been in an accident, remember? I need to be coddled."

"You need to be committed," she shot back. "To an institution for the terminally self-indulgent."

One dark eyebrow rose. "My, my. Moral judgments already? And you hardly know me."

Did she sound like a censoring maiden aunt? Probably. And why not? She needed to protect herself, just like anybody else. The feelings this man stirred in her were mixed and confusing. The undeniable charm he wore like casual clothing almost made her forget Johnny... but not quite.

She glanced at her own hand. She was always a little surprised to find the ring finger empty. She'd taken off her rings three years ago, when she'd felt ready to emerge from her widowhood and rejoin the world of man/woman relationships. She'd dated a lot at first, sure there had to be someone out there who could take Johnny's place. But gradually she'd been disillusioned.

What had happened to men, anyway? Maybe it was true. All the good ones were taken. Lately she'd preferred a pint of ice cream and a good book on Saturday nights.

"My house is on the way," she told him. "We can stop there if you like."

"Great. I just need a few minutes to pull myself together. Meeting my mother is always a harrowing experience."

And not just for him, Ann mused with a secret smile. Mrs. Sterling was not formidable like some wealthy matrons. What she was, though, was a bit strange.

Ann's little house wasn't far. She pulled down the long driveway and came to a stop at the edge of her flower garden, where Iceland poppies and ranunculuses danced in the headlights almost as brightly as they did in the midday sun. Her headlights reflected off the glass panels of the greenhouse Johnny had built for her in the backyard.

"Here we are." She got out briskly, determined to make this a quick and businesslike stop. "Come on in."

He got out more slowly and she watched him for a moment, just a bit anxious, looking for evidence of injury. But he didn't seem to be in any pain. So she turned and led the way in.

Once inside, she looked around nervously, as though Johnny's presence still lingered in the air. This was the house she and Johnny had bought together when times had been good. It was full of his touches, his repairs, his cabinetwork, his baseball on the bookcase shelf, his pictures in her bedroom. But Cam couldn't know that.

"Sit down," she offered, gesturing toward the crisp linen couch. "What would you like? I don't have anything alcoholic. I could put on a pot of coffee, or get you a cold soda from the refrigerator."

"Something very cold would be great," he drawled.

Instead of finding a seat, he wandered around her living room, touching things. "Something very cold and very tall. Anything that fizzes and has big cubes of ice floating in it. Thanks." He picked up a small figurine of dolphins leaping above waves and turned it in his hand, then went on to one of a boy and his dog. It had been Johnny's favorite piece. She watched him for a moment, biting her lip, not really sure why his scrutiny of her things made her uneasy.

Turning away, she went to the kitchen and took a
can of soda out of the refrigerator and a tall glass from
the cabinet. She hesitated before going back into the
living room. Leaning against the counter, she pressed
the cold can to her flushed cheek and closed her eyes.
Cam Sterling was back in her life.

And that was really very odd, because he didn't even
realize he'd ever been important to her. She'd only
spoken to him here and there, casually, as had every
other girl at Covington High School that year. He and
Johnny had been friends, and she'd been in the process of becoming Johnny's girl, but she knew Cam had
never really noticed her. Not the way she'd noticed
him. Even during that one, crazy night at the senior
picnic...

Shaking herself, she straightened and sighed. This
reminiscing was going to get her nowhere. She needed
the job Mrs. Sterling had offered her. She had to get
back out to the Sterling estate and hand over their one
and only son. It was all very well to dream, but there
was real life to be lived.

Cam was sitting on her linen couch and staring at
the painting on her wall. "Owl Creek?" he guessed,
as she came into the room.

She smiled in surprise and handed him his drink.
"Yes, it is. How did you recognize it..." She was
going to say "after all these years," but she caught
herself in time. Just because he remembered the setting didn't mean he remembered the senior picnic—or
the kiss in the dark. She glanced at him and saw that
she was right. There was no spark of recognition there.

He was shrugging. "I think the places of your youth
get stamped on your soul," he said softly. "I've been

living in New York City for years, but when I dream..." He smiled at her. "When I dream at night, I'm always back here, running through the hills or swimming in Skater River. Funny, isn't it?"

She stared down at him, touched by what he'd said. For so many years she'd resented him, resented the way he'd raised Johnny's hopes and then never fulfilled them. She'd come to think of him as cold and unfeeling, a handsome shell of superficiality over an empty, self-centered core. She'd forgotten some of the qualities that had attracted her to him in the first place.

Suddenly she noticed that he was watching her with a bemused look.

"Are you going to stand over me and monitor whether I finish every last drop?" he asked as though truly interested.

"I...I didn't mean to hover." She retreated to a seat across from him, then glanced at her watch. "But I do want to get going. I'm late for my appointment with your mother."

"Ah, yes. Mom does not like to be kept waiting." He laughed softly. "Well, you can blame it all on me. She's used to that."

He grinned and she found herself smiling back at him, suddenly caught in the moment, connecting. The grin slipped from his lips as their gazes clung, and when she finally tore hers away, she found herself just a bit breathless.

Damn Cam Sterling, anyway! What was it about the man that had always had this element of sensual provocation? She was too old, too experienced to fall for it again. She stared at the floor and jumped when he spoke.

"Are you married?" he asked softly.

She took a deep breath and risked another glance into his eyes. "No. Not anymore. My husband died." She said it as though it were armor that would somehow protect her from him.

"Oh," he said, slightly startled. "I'm sorry."

She couldn't stand this any longer. Getting up, she began the usual search for her car keys, hoping to coax him to get on with it. Instead, she intrigued him.

"Do I know you?" he said suddenly, making her whirl to face him again. "Something about the way you move..." He shook his head, frowning.

She knew she should tell him the truth, but somehow, thinking of bringing up Johnny and what had happened to him brought a lump to her throat, as it always did. She couldn't. Not yet. So she ignored the question.

But she gave up on urging him along. Sinking back down into the seat, she cleared her throat and tried to think of a neutral topic of conversation.

"So, you are home for a visit," she said at last. "Your mother must be pleased."

He nodded, eyes sparkling. "Well, it's not just a simple visit," he explained, pouring what was left of the soda into his glass. "Actually, it's more of a command visitation, if you know what I mean."

"I see." She thought of the old Cam and all his scrapes. "Been sent home in disgrace?" she asked, only half joking.

"In disgrace?" He looked at her quizzically. "Not at all. Why would you say a thing like that?"

She hid her smile, not sure if he was being serious.
Why indeed! The old Cam was always being sent
somewhere in disgrace. Even his year at the local high
school, instead of his usual ritzy private prep school in
the East, was considered something akin to being sen-
tenced to hard labor in Siberia. At least that was what
all the locals assumed—that he was being dumped
among them as a punishment for exotic misdeeds, the
exact nature of which were only whispered at. Cam
was just that sort of boy.

She remembered that first day of school. It had been
her freshman year. Johnny had been a senior and just
beginning to show interest. They'd walked to school
together and there was Cam Sterling, frowning at the
directory on the front lawn, trying to figure out how
to get to his first-period class. Johnny—sweet, sweet
Johnny—had dropped everything to help him. The
others had hung back, partly in awe, partly in resent-
ment against the rich kid who had come slumming
among them. But not Johnny.

Pangs of guilt shot through her with the same
blinding pain they'd had when they'd been fresh, and
she looked up quickly, afraid Cam might have noticed. Regret welled in her. Why had he come back this
way? She didn't need this. Not again.

Cam hadn't noticed anything. He was taking a long
sip of his cold drink, and when he'd finished, he continued from where they'd left off a moment before.

"Actually," he said with casual tranquility, "I've
come home to get married."

Her stomach gave a lurch and her breath caught in
her throat. "Married?" she said, and her voice
sounded tinny to her own ear. Oh hell, don't let on

that you give a hoot! And you don't. You don't. "Who . . . who is the lucky bride?"

"I don't know yet," he said as though that were the most logical response in the world and she was rather thick not to think of it. "That's exactly what I came home to find out."

She stared at him. Was he teasing her? No. He couldn't be. There was no way he could know that she might care. "I'm afraid I don't understand," she said, watching him carefully.

He stretched out his long legs before him. "You remember that prince in the Cinderella story?" He grinned. "That's me. My mother is having a ball— well, a series of balls, actually, to find me a bride." He shrugged. "My mother has always been a fairy tale fan. Now she wants to live one."

He was teasing, wasn't he? The idea was absurd.

"She's combing the hills for eligible females," he went on blithely. "I'm surprised she hasn't knocked on your door."

"Oh, I'm not eligible," she said quickly, before she thought.

He cocked one dark eyebrow. "No? Why not?"

It was obvious. She was too old, too previously married, too much a commoner for this rich, blue-blooded clan. He knew it as well as she did.

"I'm not in a marrying mood," she said lightly. "But I guess you are."

"Well, I wouldn't say that exactly. My mother is." He made a face. "I promised her years ago that I would marry by the time I was thirty-five. Well, here comes my thirty-fifth birthday, and I haven't found anyone myself. So she gets to choose someone for me.''

Ann could hardly believe her ears. She leaned forward, staring at him. "You'd actually do that? You would let your mother pick out the woman you'll spend the rest of your life with?"

He laughed shortly, leaning back, a pained expression on his handsome face. "No, now...see, you're taking this much too seriously. It's not as though I were going to stick around and live with this woman or anything like that."

She blinked. "You're not?" she said, bewildered.

"Of course not. This is purely a business arrangement. Oh, I'll probably stay long enough to do a little begetting, if you know what I mean...."

Ann didn't know whether to laugh or cry. "A little begetting? You mean...children?"

"Sure."

He was so earnest about the plan, it almost seemed credible. Almost, but not quite.

"That's the point, you see. We need someone to carry on the line and all that."

This was taking on more and more aspects of black comedy. "Right," Ann said, a tiny bit of sarcasm filtering into her tone. "Are you planning twins on the first try, or will you tarry long enough to provide for consecutive births?"

"Consecutive births?" The concept seemed to be foreign to Cam.

"They each take at least nine months you know."

"Nine months," he muttered, his brow furrowing. "You're right. You know, I had never really thought this through thoroughly."

Ann was getting into it now, enjoying herself. She was sure he was kidding, but she played along. "And what if she doesn't have a boy?"

His face mirrored his shock at her suggestion. "Things like that do happen, don't they?"

"Sure. And even worse..." She fixed him with a serious stare and said it slowly. "What if she can't get pregnant?"

He closed his eyes and leaned his head back against the couch, the picture of tragic collapse.

"Quite the little optimist, aren't you?" he complained. "It's enough to make me want to turn around and head back for New York."

Ann decided she didn't need to go into a lecture on the joys of diapering children at this stage. "Cute," she commented. "But enough of this silliness. Why are you really here?"

He opened one eye and stared at her with it. "I told you. I'm getting married." He straightened, all humor gone. "It may sound like a joke to you, but you don't have to live with the consequences."

She swallowed, hardly knowing what to say. This was crazy, and he seemed to know it. But something in his voice told her he was determined to go through with it, one way or another. And that he hated it.

"Have you finished your drink?" she asked gently. "I'm over an hour late to meet your mother."

He sighed, the smile creeping back. "You're one of those irritating people who expect others to face reality and their responsibilities, aren't you?"

His words hurt a little, but she stuck her chin out and accepted the description. "I suppose I am."

He grinned. "Good. I need a woman like you in my life." He emptied his glass and waved it in the air. "Take me home, Ann. I'm ready to face the music."

He rose and started for the kitchen with his glass and can in one hand, but before he'd taken more than a few steps, he stopped and swayed for a moment, and she was afraid he was about to lose his balance.

Ann cried out and leaped forward, catching him, using her body as a prop to hold him up. "I knew you were hurt," she said anxiously. "I'm taking you to the emergency room right now."

He was leaning on her, but the pressure wasn't as heavy as it should have been if he were in state of total collapse, and when she looked up into his face, she found his eyes as full of laughter as ever.

"It was nothing," he said softly. "I just got up too fast." His arms closed around her, his breath was warm on her cheek, and his free hand slid into her ebony hair.

"Shall we dance?" he whispered with practiced seductive technique.

For just a moment, she was shocked speechless. She'd lived this scene before—hadn't she?

No, wait a minute. She hadn't lived it. She'd only dreamed it, a long, long time ago, back when her dreams had been full of guilty thoughts of Cam Sterling, and she'd let herself imagine what it would feel like to have his long, hard body pressed to hers.

This was no dream, and yet, it had the same air of unreality to it.

"Cam!" She struggled, tearing away from him. "What are you doing?"

"I don't know, Ann." The smile faded and his eyes were searching hers. "What do you want me to do?"

She felt as though she'd just run a mile uphill. Air was hard to pull down into her lungs and her hands were shaking. Could he tell? Or was it so casual a thing with him that he was sure every woman he met wanted him?

"Come on," she said evasively, turning and leading the way out with brisk determination. "We're late."

Two

He'd known her before. He was sure of it. If only he could remember where and when.

He glanced sideways at her, watching how skillfully she handled the little van on the curves. She was pretty in a cool, elegant way, her long black hair pulled back and hanging free between her shoulder blades, her crystal blue eyes rimmed with ebony lashes, her features crisp and clean. Everything was carefully in order, not a hair out of place. Was her life that fully under control, as well?

His wide mouth stretched just the tiniest bit into a quiet smile. He didn't think so. Something told him that her careful outward appearance was set up as a shield to hide another person entirely. There was a reserve there, the sort of reserve that set up a challenge and made a man want to prove he could overcome it.

But he was going to resist in this case. He wasn't sure exactly what she had meant when she'd told him she wasn't eligible for his marriage mart, but he did know she wasn't the type he and his mother were looking for. She was too smart, too much a person in her own right. She would never go for the scheme his mother had in mind.

His madcap, irrepressible mother. He dreaded seeing her. He could hardly wait to see her. In all the world, that woman was the only one who had ever put the fear of God into him. And yet, he adored her, would do almost anything for her.

Obviously. How many sons would let their mother dictate these marriage terms for them? The very thought of marriage chilled him. Marriage hadn't worked out for many of the males of his family. And the one time he himself had come close had been such a disaster. Dusty's face swam before his eyes, but he shook her image away, not even wincing. Marriage would be no picnic.

But he owed this to his mother. This time, he would have to bite the bullet and go through with it.

They whisked past the wreck of his rented sports car, taking Outlaw's Pass at the proper speed and having no trouble at all. Neither of them spoke as the crumpled mass of metal rushed in and out of the headlights.

He turned to look at her again, more obvious this time, studying her profile. She glanced at him.

"What is it?"

He smiled at her prickly response to his interest. "I'm trying to figure out where we knew each other before," he told her.

Her startled look told him all he needed to know. She remembered all right. Why wasn't she volunteering the information on her own?

"Ever been to New York?" he asked.

She shook her head. "Never."

"Well, that narrows it down. How old are you?"

She seemed to need all her attention for her driving. "That's a question you're not supposed to ask women," she muttered.

"I just want to pin you down." He threw his head back and mused. "Could it have been my Sunday school class when I was ten years old?" He glanced at her. "No. I don't think so." She still didn't respond, and he went on.

"Maybe dance class, when they tried to teach us all how to act with the opposite sex. All I remember learning was that spiders made girls scream louder than lizards did. My friend Andy and I tested that theory thoroughly." He sighed. "We should have published the results while they were fresh. We might have made quite a name for ourselves in the scientific world."

At least he had her smiling. He leaned a little closer. "So tell me, Ann. Where was it? Were you at the University of Chicago while I was there going to graduate school? I've got it! You worked in the school library, didn't you?"

She shook her head. "I've never been out of California," she admitted.

"Ah-hah. Then it had to be...high school? But you couldn't be old enough."

He was getting close. He could tell by the evasive look in her face. "Who can remember that far back?"

she said dismissively, glancing at him, then quickly away again. She took a deep breath and continued in a slightly higher voice. "Anyway, I'd rather talk about you and this crazy plan to play out your Cinderella routine."

He knew what she was doing and that she knew he knew. But he merely nodded, allowing her to go ahead. She obviously didn't want to admit they'd met before, which made him all the more determined to ferret out the truth. But there were other ways to get at it.

"It's a battle plan my mother is rather fond of," he said serenely. "But I can tell you don't agree."

She shook her head. "I don't understand why a man like you would need this sort of thing. I mean, what have you been doing all these years? Haven't you had any contact with any females on your own?"

"Well, of course." He gave her a wounded look. "I know plenty of women. I like women." He shrugged. "But marriage...I don't know much about that. One person, forever. No more variety. No more thrill of the chase." He sighed wearily. "It seems so brutal to do that to a man. I've never been able to face the prospect on my own."

She might have known he would grow up to be a self-centered, if somewhat charming, individual. It was odd to think he'd never married. How many women had tried their best to snag him? Hundreds, probably. Poor things. And now one was to be chosen to wear the lucky gold ring. Poor thing again. After all, marrying Cam would be no picnic. He'd been open about his lack of interest in the institution. All he wanted was a baby to carry on the Sterling name and make his mother happy. What a life that would be.

"Maybe things will have a fairy-tale ending," she said softly. "Maybe you'll fall in love with someone, just like the prince fell for Cinderella."

"Clumsy people 'fall' all the time," he said, his voice light and careless. "I'm more likely to crash. Hadn't you noticed?"

His words were cynical, but when she glanced at him she thought she saw something else in his face, something wistful, as though he were yearning after an enigma. As quickly as she thought she saw it, the look was gone, and the road reclaimed her attention.

The large stone pillars that signaled the entrance to the Sterling estate loomed ahead and she slowed to make the turn.

"How about you?" he asked, breaking the silence. "What did you think of marriage?"

That startled her just a bit. Most people, once they heard her husband was dead, avoided mentioning marriage or anything associated with it, as though she wouldn't remember Johnny if they didn't bring it up. But Cam Sterling was not most people. She would have to keep that in mind.

She glanced at him and gave a general answer to his question. "A good marriage is a wonderful thing."

"Sure it is. Did you have one?"

His audacity left her gasping. "That is none of your business!"

He looked at her again. "Oops. Sorry." Reaching out, he touched her arm. "We don't have to talk about it."

They'd reached the top of the long driveway and she brought the car to a stop with a jerk before the huge colonial mansion. This man could drive her crazy in no time. Now she had left him with the impression that her marriage had been unhappy—and that wasn't true. But how could she erase the mistake, without going overboard in the other direction and arousing his curiosity?

Even if she'd had a plan, it was too late to put it into action. Cam was already out of the van, bounding around to her side as though he'd never been in an accident in his life, yanking open her door and crying, "Wow, look at this place. It's great to be home!"

The butler—or at any rate, Ann supposed he was something of the sort—came out onto the front portico and frowned at them severely.

"May I enquire as to your business here?" he asked in a pinched tone.

Cam and Ann looked at one another. He'd pulled her up out of the driver's seat, but still had his arm around her shoulders.

"The old family retainer doesn't seem to recognize you," she whispered.

"Old family retainer, hell," he responded cheerfully. "My mother's never kept any employee beyond six months that I know of. It's a revolving door around here. They just stay long enough to gather references to use at houses where the employers do things a little more . . . normally. I've never seen this man before in my life."

She poked him with an elbow. "Then tell him who you are, before he pulls out the shotgun," she hissed, her attention on the butler's darkening frown.

"We don't loan out the telephone here," he was pronouncing threateningly, waving his arm as if to ward them off. "So if your vehicle has broken down, you'll have to push it back toward where you came from."

Cam turned to Ann again, his face perplexed. "Where exactly did we come from?" he asked.

"Cam!" she urged, poking him again. "Tell the nice man who you are!"

He made a face, obviously reluctant to let this game go. Sighing, he turned back to the glowering butler.

"Listen," he said, his voice suddenly that of the man in charge again. "Can you read?" He pointed out the sign on the side of Ann's van. "Surely you knew Mrs. Sterling was expecting the caterer tonight. I don't think she'll be pleased to hear about this reception you've given her."

The butler squinted at the sign, but his face didn't soften. "Well, why didn't you say so in the first place?" he grumbled, turning back toward the doorway. "Come on in, then. Though I must say you're almost two hours late, and I wouldn't blame Madam a bit if she sent the two of you packing—"

He was never able to finish his sentence as a scream ripped the air, stunning them all. Mrs. Sterling had been coming down the wide interior stairway when she caught sight of her only son on the front steps. She cried out. She flung her arms wide. And she lost her footing, came down with a thump, and began to descend the stairway on her backside.

Luckily, she was wearing a hostess gown of something slippery that looked like satin, so the ride down was smoother than it might have been. Two or three strides of Cam's long legs put him in place to catch her before she hit bottom. He tossed her up into his arms and hugged her close and she clung to his neck.

Both mother and son acted as though it were the most natural way of meeting in the world, laughing and hugging and saying the things people do when they haven't seen each other for months and months. The love between the two of them was palpable, and it touched Ann.

Suddenly she became aware that the butler was standing beside her, watching, as well. She turned to look at him and found that she was also being scrutinized by the man's glittering black eyes.

"I didn't think the young Sterling was married to the caterer," he said suspiciously.

"He's not." Ann grinned at him, the urge to be impudent irresistible. "You'd better get the family straight if you plan to keep this job."

He sniffed and rolled his eyes. "They're all batty," he muttered, shaking his head as he shuffled off.

"Batty" wasn't exactly the descriptive word Ann would have chosen, but there was no denying the Sterlings were odd. They came from old money and that sometimes seemed to produce descendants with very individual ideas of behavior. As Ann remembered it, Cam's father had been an amateur archaeologist, prone to walking around the grounds in a pith helmet with a shovel over his shoulder. He had died ten years before, leaving his estate in the hands of his wife, Evelyn Sterling. And then, of course, there was Cam. But he had been wheeling and dealing in the corporate boardrooms of New York for years and few thought he would ever come back to live in the old mansion on the hill.

Cam finally put his mother down and the two of them turned back to look at Ann. Mrs. Sterling was frowning, not sure how Ann fit into things, but once the accident was explained, she wrung Ann's hand in gratitude a few dozen times and exclaimed over her son, touching him often as though to make sure he was all in one piece.

"You promised to call your family doctor," Ann reminded Cam, who made a face at her.

But it was too late. Mrs. Sterling took up the cry, using the telephone in the hall to do the job herself, and then ringing for the butler.

"Where is that man? Maxwell!" she called out when the bell didn't seem to do the trick. "Maxwell, come carry Mr. Sterling's bags up."

Cam dropped a kiss on the top of his mother's silver head. "I can carry them myself," he told her gruffly. "Now you go into the parlor and talk to Ann about party preparations. I'll get settled and be down in a little while." His smile warmed Ann. "Don't run away too soon," he said softly as he brushed past her. "I still want to talk to you."

Mrs. Sterling watched him leave with a fond smile on her carefully painted lips, but once he was out of sight, her face changed. She got down to business.

"Shall we go into the kitchen?" she suggested, sweeping Ann with a sharp look before turning to lead the way. "I do think that would be more appropriate."

Ann noted the fact that she'd been demoted from the parlor, as Cam had suggested, to the kitchen,

which was where "help" went. She grinned as she
followed the older woman through the maze of hall-
ways, wondering if Cam would be able to find her
again. Perhaps not. And wouldn't that be for the best?
Her grin faded.

The kitchen was a wonderful place—all soft, oiled
wood and shining white ceramic tile. The pots had
gleaming copper bottoms and stainless steel utensils
hung from racks. It would be a dream setting for the
things Ann loved to do. She looked about with pleasure, touching things.

They sat at a long, butcher block table and Mrs.
Sterling spread out charts and lists to explain what she
had in mind for the series of parties she was giving
over the next six weeks. There was nothing particu-
larly special about them, as far as Ann could see. She
was surprised they couldn't be handled with the
kitchen staff Mrs. Sterling must have on hand at any
given time, but then she remembered what Cam had
said about the turnover rate. Perhaps there wasn't
anyone experienced enough to be trusted at the moment.

"Of course, everyone will be in costume," Mrs.
Sterling said serenely at one point.

Ann blinked. "Costume? You mean . . . guests will
be asked to dress up?"

"Certainly." She smiled whimsically. She'd once
been a beauty and was still a very attractive woman,
with silver hair and huge brown eyes. Her skin was
creamy, though lined. An odd combination of so-
phistication and dreaminess, she was interesting, if a
little disconcerting.

"Each party will have a different theme," she went on. "A Midsummer Night's Dream, a Spanish fiesta, a circus scene, a Russian rendezvous, a Roaring Twenties night and a beach party. Those are just some of the suggestions. We'll provide costumes here. They will only have to choose once they arrive." She dismissed that with a wave of her hand. "But you won't have to worry about that. You will only be concerned with the food."

Ann was beginning to realize arrangements for these parties might not be as simple as she'd assumed. "You'll want the food coordinated with the themes, though," she noted doubtfully.

"Oh, of course."

Of course. Ann had sudden visions of spending every waking hour for six weeks ensconced right here in the Sterling kitchen, frantically making completely unique entrées for hordes of picky guests. Maybe she didn't need this job so badly after all.

But she didn't have time to register her unease with Mrs. Sterling. Suddenly Cam was framed by the large double doorway.

"Guess what," he said to Ann, his eyes brimming with amusement. "I found you."

In his hand he held a familiar-looking book. Ann had to look twice before she realized it was the high school yearbook from her freshman year. Shock jolted through her.

"No!" she cried, leaping to her feet and reaching for the book, half laughing, half aghast. "Don't look at that picture."

"It's a wonderful picture," he said, holding it just out of her reach and grinning at her with devilish glee. "You looked great in pigtails."

"Those aren't pigtails." She tried in vain to grab the book from him, only ending up much too close to him, her body straining against his as she reached high. Suddenly she realized what this must look like, and remembered who else was in the room. "Oh." She pulled away, reddening, looking at Cam's mother sheepishly. "I'm sorry, Mrs. Sterling. I . . ."

Cam saved the day with his usual grace, coming into the room and sinking into a chair at the long table, just around the corner from where Ann was retaking her place. "Mother, Ann and I went to high school together."

Mrs. Sterling's stunned look faded, giving way to disapproval. "Oh, that dreadful high school."

"It wasn't dreadful at all. It was a great place. I had a wonderful time."

"You did nothing but get into scrapes your father and I had to get you out of."

Cam blinked with all innocence. "That's what I said. I had a wonderful time." He smiled at Ann and she bit her lip, trying hard not to let his charm wear away her reserve.

A wonderful time. He'd enjoyed Covington High, and then he'd cast it aside as casually as he might trade in an old car for a new model, completely forgetting all the friends he'd made. Did he have any idea of the heartbreak he'd left behind? She doubted it. Still, that didn't excuse what he'd done. That didn't excuse the way he'd hurt Johnny. She had to remember that. And remember how easily he could hurt again.

"Oh, by the way, Mother," he was saying, "Grandma Westin is on the phone. Why don't you go on into the parlor to take the call?" He turned his gaze back on Ann. "I have a job to do here with this young lady."

Mrs. Sterling noted the look he was giving the caterer and frowned, rising with reluctance. But once up, she left quickly. It was obvious Grandma Westin was a force to be reckoned with. In the meantime, Ann had Cam and his overactive curiosity to deal with.

She looked down at the book, then up into his dark eyes. "Please don't ever look at that picture again," she pleaded, only half serious.

He slapped the book and grinned. "Never fear, there's more here to ponder." He flipped it open. "Let's look in the index and find out all the clubs you were in."

The potential humiliation of having him see her picture in an apron holding a piglet for Future Farmers of America was just too great. She lunged for the book. He stopped her with a well-aimed grab that had her practically in his arms.

"Cam!" She looked up into his eyes, caught by the laughter, intrigued by the warmth, and for a long moment, she didn't draw away.

"Come on," he said at last, touching her hair lightly. "Let's just look at some pictures and stir up some memories. Okay?"

It would be silly to protest, wouldn't it? She'd feel like a fool. But still, stirring up memories was the last thing she wanted to do. Memories had barbs.

He tugged her closer, moving her chair until it almost touched his. "Why didn't you tell me?" he asked softly, his gaze searching hers.

She looked away. "We...we really didn't know each other," she said. "I was just a freshman. You were a senior."

"But I remember you." He studied her profile. "Why do I remember you?"

She felt a flush spreading across her face again. The last thing in the world she wanted was for him to remember.

"Let's look at the pictures," she said, changing tactics. Anything to get his mind off her.

They began to shuffle through the past, leafing through photos of the Homecoming queen, the football games, the Spring Sing. Dread began to build up in Ann's chest. It had been years since she'd looked through her copy of this book. But she knew there was a huge picture of Johnny coming up. He'd been the star pitcher of the baseball team that year, and they'd won the league championship and had done pretty well in regionals, too. What would he say when he got to the picture of Johnny? What would he remember then?

"Margi Caukins," he mused, smiling at the picture of the Junior Prom queen. "I dated her for a while. She took me skinny dipping in Kramer's reservoir." He looked up at Ann. "Whatever happened to Margi?"

"Five babies and a management job for a motel chain. She's living out on Caballo Road if you want to visit her." Ann almost grinned to think of what Jeff,

Margi's bodybuilding husband, would think of Cam coming to call.

But Cam was shaking his head. "Some memories are best left with the dusty patina of the past to protect them," he said. He turned the page and there was Johnny, a baseball glove in his hand, a cap pulled low over his sweet eyes, staring out at them from beyond forever.

Ann's heart stopped in her chest. Cam was still, as well.

"Johnny," he breathed at last. "Wait a minute. That's...that's Johnny Dupree. He and I were best friends my senior year." Cam shook his head in wonderment. "Lord, but he was a great guy. One of the best. I can't believe we never got together again." He looked up at Ann, smiling. "Now there's someone I'd like to see. Whatever happened to him? Where is he now?"

The answer stuck in her throat and Cam's face changed. Dropping the book, he grasped her by her upper arms. "What is it?" he asked quickly. "What is it, Ann? Are you all right?"

She nodded and forced out the words. "Johnny...Johnny was my husband."

Cam frowned. "You mean he's..." He hesitated as the full implication sank in.

She nodded, her lips set. "He's dead."

"Dead." Cam sat back, stunned, and his face was an open book as reactions flashed across it. She could see what he was thinking—how much he'd once cared for Johnny, how big a loss it was that Johnny was no longer in the world. Despite everything, it hurt Cam.

That was interesting. As far as he was concerned, Johnny might as well have died the day he left the valley for college in the East. After all, he'd never done anything to contact any of them again. And when Johnny had reached his most desperate moment, when he'd actually cried out for help, Cam had ignored him. So what did it matter to him that Johnny was dead?

And yet, it did. She could see that it did. And despite everything, that touched her.

"What happened?" he asked, his voice hoarse.

She crossed her arms in front of her, holding in the ache that always came when she let herself remember. "It was...cancer. It happened very quickly. It was over in a matter of weeks."

His arm came around her, pulling her into his warmth, and she wanted to melt into his comfort.

But she pushed away from Cam's embrace. If she let him hold her she would cry, and that would be ridiculous. "It was almost ten years ago now," she said brightly, managing a brittle smile. "I mean, it's not as though we hadn't all done our mourning at the time." She nodded toward the book. "Go on. You don't have to stop."

He stared at her for a moment, then turned back to the annual and began turning pages. But she could see that his attention was no longer on the pictures. He was remembering, thinking about Johnny.

Luckily there wasn't much about her he could possibly remember. There had only been that one incident at the senior picnic. But a man like Cam was, with all his experience with women—there was no way he would remember that. She began to relax and let herself remember it for just a moment.

The senior picnic. It was held the night before graduation at Owl Creek. The seniors and their dates built a huge bonfire and danced in the sand. The highlight had been the traditional senior kiss at midnight. Johnny had gone to pick up more sodas with a group of other boys and hadn't returned yet. Just before he'd left, he'd laughingly told Cam to "take care of my girl for me."

Now someone was calling out the time, counting down to midnight, and suddenly, there was Cam, sliding in beside her where she sat in the shadows, on the old fallen log. He was smiling that smile that sent hearts spinning all over campus, and saying smoothly, "I can't let Johnny's girl be left out of this. After all, I promised him I'd take good care of you, didn't I?"

Midnight came and his hand captured her chin, coaxing her face toward his. She could hardly breathe. She didn't think about Johnny. She didn't think about the ethics of the situation. She didn't think at all.

Kissing Cam was a dream come true, and it all happened so fast, with no warning. She'd had a crush on Cam since the first day of school, but she'd never even allowed herself to hope that anything would come of it. He was like a movie actor or a rock star—someone to be worshiped from afar, someone unattainable. She'd been going steady with Johnny for almost a month by then, and she liked him a lot. But Cam Sterling . . . that was something else again.

And suddenly here he was, kissing her, thrilling her, sending her into a spin like nothing she'd ever experienced before. His lips were smooth and warm and he tasted minty. Her mouth seemed to melt under his, and the kiss deepened, taking on a life of its own. A distant church bell tolled twelve times, but they weren't listening. The kiss went on and on.

And then it was over and they were drawing back. Ann stared at Cam, stunned by what they'd shared. He was staring back, not saying a word, looking at her as though he were really seeing her for the first time. And then the car drove up with the sodas and Johnny was back, and Cam faded into the crowd.

She never saw him again. Until she found him in a wreck near Outlaw's Pass.

"Well, you two, I hope you've concluded your reminiscences." Mrs. Sterling was back, bustling into the room dramatically. "Cameron, Dr. Michaels called back to say he would be here in about an hour. Why don't you go lie down, dear, and rest?"

Cam gave his mother a fleeting smile, but he didn't move, and she sat down and pulled out her charts again, as though he'd left as she'd suggested. Ann only half heard the things she was saying. Her mind was full of indecision. Should she take this job? Or should she walk away and avoid Cam and the problems he represented? She glanced at him from time to time, disturbed by his moody gaze, which was fixed, mainly, on her. What was he thinking? And why did her heart still beat faster when her eyes met his?

"Well, then. When will you be able to start?" Mrs. Sterling raised her eyebrows as she waited for Ann's answer.

Ann hesitated. This was it. Should she? Or shouldn't she? She glanced at Cam. His stare was intense. Shivering, she tore her gaze away and looked at his mother. "You know, Mrs. Sterling," she began, "I'm not sure..."

"Take the job, Ann."

She looked back at Cam, startled. He was still staring in that odd way.

"Please take the job," he repeated. "I'll help you in any way I can."

Mrs. Sterling shook her head as though to clear it. "Cameron, darling," she began.

But he didn't let her get started. "She'll need a room here at the house, Mother. There will be a lot to do. She'll be busy twenty-four hours a day. She'd better be here where she can stay on top of things."

"Oh, Cameron, I don't see—"

"Mother." His voice was the "boss" voice again, steel-hard, rock-firm. "I think it would be best."

Mrs. Sterling fluttered in agitation. "Well, if you really think so, dear..."

Ann sat very still. She hadn't said a word. It seemed decisions were being made for her. That was unusual. She was a cool, careful businesswoman who usually made plans decisively and didn't let anyone else run roughshod over her. She knew it would be best for all concerned if she bowed out of this job and left Cam to his wife-hunting without her help. The speeches to say just that kept forming in her head, but somehow she couldn't quite get them to her lips.

She watched in a haze as Mrs. Sterling and Cam talked back and forth, saying something about Monday, something about landscapers and decorators. And then Mrs. Sterling was leaving the room and she was alone with Cam and it seemed to be decided. She was going to be the Sterling caterer for the duration.

Cam reached across the table and took her hand in his. "Do you feel just a little railroaded?" he asked.

"Sorry. But I think we can work well together. Give it a try. Okay?"

She never could resist him. Still, she resented it. She stared into his dark eyes. "Do you always get your way?" she asked softly.

His grin was unapologetic. "Pretty much." He sobered, searching her eyes. "We never dated, did we?"

"No."

"That's right. You were Johnny's girl."

She pulled her hand from his and rose. "I'd better get home," she said, starting for the back door instinctively. "Goodbye."

He came along with her, though she hadn't wanted that. She felt him, heard him, but didn't look around until they were outside and he came up next to her. He walked alongside her, not saying anything at all. The cool night air seemed to slap her face.

"Did you and Johnny have any children?" he asked at last.

She didn't want him to talk about Johnny anymore. Johnny was hers, not his. He'd given up his right to Johnny long ago. She closed her eyes for a quick moment, knowing she was being illogical.

"No," she forced herself to answer calmly. "We never felt we were quite ready. And then . . . it was too late."

They reached her van and she stopped, turning to face him, leaning back against the door. Now that she was here it was hard to drive off and leave him.

"That's the way I've always felt—not ready," he told her, his face dark and shadowed in the night. "And now, I guess I'm probably going to have to have a child anyway."

He spoke as though a child were something one decided to buy, like a VCR or a guard dog. But her momentary reaction to that was dimmed as she realized what his words really meant. He didn't always get his own way after all. He was set. He was going to carry on this crazy marriage auction. And he was prepared to go ahead and father a child. But it wasn't his idea. He was doing it for someone else—his mother, she supposed. Or maybe for the Sterling family name. Whatever. At least it meant he was capable of doing something outside of his own interest. For some reason, that cheered her.

"I had better get going." She turned and reached for the door handle.

His hand closed around her upper arm. "Ann...you will be back, won't you?"

She looked up into his eyes, impudence coming to the fore again. "I'll think it over," she said pertly. "After all, I haven't signed a contract, have I?"

"No," he agreed, moving closer. "But how about this in the meantime?"

Before she realized what was happening, he'd pulled her close to his long, hard body and had smothered her lips with his own. She gasped in surprise, and he took complete control, his mouth hot on hers, his kiss strong and urgent.

It was too intense for a first kiss. There was no exploration, no tentative questioning. This kiss was rich with mature desire, hard with the demand for recognition, seductive with the technique of a practiced lover. She had never been kissed this way before. It was both frightening and tantalizing, a promise of danger, a hint of ecstasy, a declaration of attraction. No first kiss should be so bold.

But then she remembered—it wasn't a first kiss at all.

He drew back, looking down into her face, his breath coming quickly, just as hers was. Her mouth tingled from contact with his, and her heart was beating very fast. She couldn't speak. She could only stare up at him in wonder.

"I haven't forgotten when we did this before, Ann," he said huskily, running a finger down the side of her cheek. "I don't believe you have, either."

She turned blindly, reaching for the door handle again, and this time she managed to open the door and get herself into the seat. She didn't say a word to him as she gunned the engine and drove off down the long driveway. Looking back, she could see him still standing there in the shadows.

Three

"I'm sorry, Mrs. Sterling. I can't do it. Your son will have to find another playmate to help him while away the summer days."

Ann stared with awesome determination at her own reflection in the pane of greenhouse glass. She was marvelous—chin high, eyes cool and assessing, shoulders set—a fit opponent for any contest of wills.

Of course, one had to ignore the huge, filthy gardening gloves on her hands, the torn yellow shorts with flower shears hanging out of one pocket, the smudge of dirt clinging to her cheek and the pine needles bristling in her hair. Not to mention the fact that Mrs. Sterling was miles away happily puttering in her own garden and unable to hear a word Ann said. This was just a rehearsal, after all, a sort of "things I would say if I had the nerve" session.

"You see, Mrs. Sterling," she went on sternly, star-
tling away a blue jay who had been thinking about
landing on her row of freshly planted tomato seed-
lings. "I am a professional caterer, not a procurer, not
even a matchmaker. You want to dangle your son before the female population of the world like some large
piece of tempting bait, you be my guest. But as for me,
I'm not biting!"

"Well, good for you." The voice from behind made
her whirl, gloved hands to her face in horror. Cam
grinned. "I like a woman who doesn't bite. One
doesn't feel the need for quite as much protective
clothing that way, don't you agree?"

She hadn't heard him drive up and come around the
house. He was dressed in light blue slacks and a navy
blue polo shirt, looking as though he were about to
take the helm on the high seas. Why did he have to be
so completely gorgeous?

She tried to smile, and at the same time, she wondered how much dirt she'd put on her face in her moment of surprise on hearing his voice. "I . . . I don't
usually talk to myself like that."

"No? Why not? I always do." He took a step forward and pulled a handkerchief from his pocket at the
same time, then reached out to gently dust her face. "I
find I like my own answers so much better than I like
the ones others give me."

She dutifully closed her eyes and let him clean her
face, feeling silly, but just a bit taken care of, as well.
When he'd finished, she opened her eyes and found he
was still standing there, looking down at her. Flash-
ing him a quick smile, she pulled away and began to
yank off the gloves.

"What did you hear?" she asked, avoiding his eyes as she dropped the gloves and the flower shears into a bin beside the greenhouse. "How long were you standing there listening to me?"

"Just long enough to hear you vow never to bite again. Why?" His gaze sharpened. "Did I miss the good parts?"

She gave him a long, searching look, then turned and started toward the house, knowing he would follow without having to be asked. Despite her reservations, she was going to go out to the Sterling estate and try her hand at this catering job—even though it was overwhelmingly against her better judgment.

"I'm not ready to go yet," she informed him over her shoulder. It had been decided that Cam would drive her to the estate and she would have the use of Sterling vehicles. She was sure this was because Mrs. Sterling didn't want a van with her catering logo on the side to sit around cluttering up her driveway. But what if it were also so that she couldn't escape so easily? She had her own suspicions as to whose idea this was.

"I can see that," Cam answered.

"You're early."

"I know. There's nothing to do out at my house. So I thought I'd just—"

She turned, one hand on the knob to the back door, and stared at him. "Nothing to do! There are the horses and the swimming pool and a billiard room and tennis courts and an indoor bowling alley."

He shrugged disarmingly and gave her the benefit of his abundant charm. "Yeah. But there's no one to do any of that with."

So it was just as she'd suspected. Cam wanted a playmate. She opened the door and went on into the kitchen, wiping her feet on the mat and muttering, "I was never under the impression that you were the type who needed constant companionship."

He was coming in right behind her. She glanced at him, struck by how out of place his expensive casualness looked in her ceramic tile and basket-weave kitchen. Was she going to look just as out of place in his big old mansion? What a question. Of course she was.

"You're right," he was saying. "I never have been that type. But you know...?" He looked at her as though he was totally bewildered by this new concept himself. "I feel a change of life-style coming on."

She stared at him for another long moment, then nodded briskly and started into the hall toward her bedroom. "Of course. That's what this is all about, isn't it? You'll be changing your life pretty drastically."

"Well...sort of."

Stopping before her dresser, she pulled the pins out of her hair and raked through it for pine needles. He stood in the doorway, leaning on the jamb. She probably shouldn't have let him follow her to her bedroom this way. It was hardly appropriate. But somehow she didn't feel the least bit awkward about his presence. He wasn't threatening. Not right now.

While there was something dangerous in the fact that they had known each other before, there was also something intimate about it, as though they really did have a shared connection that couldn't be severed. On a certain level, she knew him as she knew no other.

She glanced at him, noting the way his blond hair curled about his ear. She liked that.

"Wouldn't it be nice if you could find a wife who shared all your interests?" she commented dryly. "Somebody who could play all your little games with you?"

He seemed to like that idea. "You mean some dandy gal who would sit and sip cold beer and watch football games in an old undershirt with me?" His eyes shone with interest. "And during halftime, she would go out and catch a few passes in the mud. Say, you know, you might just have something there. How do I find a woman like that?"

She couldn't help it. She laughed. There was something so open and honest about him. He seemed to let it all hang out, no matter what it made him look like.

And yet, that wasn't true at all. There was a guarded quality in the recesses of his eyes. His candor was on the surface, and was probably little more than a ruse to camouflage what was really going on deep inside.

She looked away, reaching for her robe. "You don't want a wife. You want a son."

"Good Lord, you are a perceptive one, aren't you? Maybe...maybe I could just get the kids without having to marry anybody. I suppose I could adopt. And then..." He looked as though a brilliant idea had just occurred to him. "I could hire you to come take care of them."

She swung around and glared at him. "No way. I have no experience in taking care of children. I don't want the job."

He spoke softly in a way that made her look hard at him again, trying to get by that protective screen in his eyes. "But you could do it if you tried. You could do most anything you put your mind to. I can tell."

She searched, but he wasn't about to let her in. "How can you tell?" she asked. "You don't really know anything about me."

"I've been responsible for hiring and firing staff for quite a few years, and I've developed something of an instinct. I can tell."

Their gazes held as the seconds ticked by and a slight flutter of panic invaded Ann's chest. Was this the way it was going to be? If so, she couldn't do it. She couldn't go and live in proximity to this man. It would drive her crazy.

She turned toward the bathroom, robe in hand. "I'm going to take a quick shower," she informed him over her shoulder. "If you have something to do, I'll be ready in about half an hour."

"I'll wait here," he said, watching as she closed the door with a decisive snap.

He hesitated, half expecting her to come back out and order him to leave the house while she showered. But then he heard the water running and knew she was otherwise engaged. The thought of her standing naked under the shower made him smile with pleasure, and he straightened, looking around the room.

Her packed bags sat by the door. So she really was coming. He hadn't been sure. His gaze moved on.

Ann's decorating was just as down-to-earth and utilitarian as he would have expected. Her thick bedspread was white with navy blue stripes, with fat checkered pillows at the head. The dresser and dressing table were of some matching dark wood and looked antique. Navy blue curtains fluttered in the

breeze of the open window. Two pictures of spring
flowers complemented the fresh nasturtiums in a cut
glass vase on the dresser. And on the table beside the
bed stood a picture of Johnny.

Cam walked over and sat on the bed before taking
the picture in his hands and staring down at the handsome face. This Johnny was older than the one he had
known. The face seemed darker, more serious. Trouble shadowed the eyes and worry shaped the set of the
brows. The mouth was set in a firm line that could
have meant resolution, or the beginnings of despair.
It was a disturbing picture. He wondered why Ann
would want it by her bed. What did she want to be reminded of?

She still loves him, he thought. My God. Hadn't it
been ten years? And she still loved him. He must have
been quite a guy to have inspired that sort of love.

Another picture, shoved behind a stack of books,
caught his eye, and he picked it up, too. This one was
of Johnny and Ann on their wedding day, their faces
shining with happiness, looking much more as he had
known them. Ann was radiant. They both looked so
young. He stared at the picture, remembering the kiss
at the senior class picnic.

He'd been pretty new to kissing himself in those
days. He'd had girls chasing after him since junior
high, but he hadn't paid a whole lot of attention.
Soccer and basketball and his buddies had been all-
important to him. Then, suddenly, kissing had entered the picture, and once he'd really tried it, taught
by little Cassie Thornbecker, he found out the truth—
kissing was great. So that was what girls were for. Not
a bad idea at all.

At least, that was what he'd believed at the time, he thought with a rueful grin. He knew better than to express himself that way these days.

Still, kissing had been just for fun, and for that vague lustful buzz it gave you, until that night at the senior picnic. He'd kissed Ann that night. There had been something different about that kiss, something full and rich and laden with emotions he'd never tapped before. It had startled him, made him look at her twice. Even so, he'd walked off and hardly thought of her again.

He could recall it so clearly, that startled burst of knowledge, that certainty that he had found something good and pure and worth having. How young he had been to just walk away and leave it behind with hardly a regret. He supposed it was because of the time, the place, the circumstances. There had been so much of life waiting before him at that time. The potential had seemed never ending.

"What a jerk I was," he muttered, turning the wedding picture in his hands. "How could I have thrown away everything that was valuable to me? How could I walk away from Ann's kiss, forget Johnny, leave all those people behind and hardly think of any of them again?"

Ten years. Fifteen years. How did it go so fast? How could he have let Johnny slip away? What had he been doing with his life that was so important he couldn't take the time to look up old friends?

After putting both pictures down, he stretched out on Ann's bed and waited, listening to the soothing sound of the shower, letting questions fill his mind.

She was in her robe when she finally came out, and she looked startled to find him lying on her bed with his arms behind his head, as though he had every right to be there.

He stared at her. She was constantly surprising him. Here she was, fresh out of the shower, nothing but clean woman. To his amazement, the sight of her affected him in a visceral way that was strong and unambiguous. He wanted her. It was as elemental as that.

She looked rather regal with her hair all wet and slicked back from her face. He'd seldom seen a woman this way before. Most of the women he went out with were very careful to always look their best around him, protected by makeup and hairstylists and all that money could buy. But not Ann. She was as real, as genuine an article as Johnny had been. What you saw was what you got.

She frowned and took a swipe at his leg. "Hey, you. That's my bed. You get off."

He rolled to his side, propping up his head with an elbow, and grinned at her. "That's not very friendly. I rather thought you might be willing to share for a while."

Their gazes connected, but he was careful not to let her see that there was an underlying intention to his teasing. Still, she was defensive, as though she knew exactly what he was thinking.

"Sorry. I don't share much that's personal to me." She tossed her wet hair back and glared at him. "Do I have to give you a lecture on what I will and won't do out there at the Sterling estate? Do I really have to explain to you that my working for you gives you no

right to expect any sort of...relationship or...or..."
Why was it so difficult to say the word? "I'm not hiring on as a playmate."

"Playmate! Why, Ann, you shock me." His frown
of outrage might have been completely convincing if
she hadn't known him better. "Nothing could be further from my mind. I'm a serious man. I have come
home on a serious mission. A mission from which
nothing shall deter me." His free arm flung out dramatically. "My course is set. My sails are full. What
was it Columbus said? 'Sail on!'"

The corners of her mouth were threatening to give
way to laughter. "Your sails are full of hot air," she
muttered, holding it back with all her might. "I'm
going to be busy. I won't have time to play."

He looked utterly mournful as he contemplated life
without a playmate. "But...you will talk to me, won't
you?"

She raised an eyebrow skeptically. "Now and then."

"I don't want you to feel duty-bound or anything
like that. Maybe just a friendly chat over breakfast in
the morning."

"Possibly."

His grin was coming back into his eyes. "Perhaps a
game of checkers in the evening?"

She frowned. "I don't think—"

"A ride before breakfast? A swim after lunch?"

"No!" She threw down her towel for emphasis.
"You're one of those 'give me an inch and I'll take a
mile' sort of people, aren't you?"

He shook his head as though she'd disappointed
him. "Have you ever noticed how often you tend to
categorize people? You do it all the time. You're

constantly analyzing my behavior and sticking parts of me into different little pigeonholes. Stereotyping, that's what you're doing. You're stereotyping me.''

''I'm doing no such thing.''

''Prove it. Give me a chance.''

She wasn't really sure what he was asking a chance for, but she was certain she didn't want to find out right now.

''I'll give you a chance to get out of here so I can get dressed,'' she told him firmly. ''Go on. Scat.''

He laughed softly as he rose to his feet. She held the door for him and he went by her slowly, leaning close as though to take in the scent of her freshly washed hair.

He glanced back as she closed the door, getting a glimpse of her profile, with Johnny's bedside picture in the background. Johnny's girl. That was what she had been. Was she still?

The Sterling mansion looked medieval in the bright light of day, ancient but idealized. Ann found herself shuddering as they went in through the gates.

Cam noticed. ''Think we ought to put up one of those signs, 'Abandon hope all ye who enter here,' or something like that? Just as a warning to visitors.''

Ann made a face. ''I just got a slight chill. I didn't mean to insult you.''

She looked at the wooded area inside the gates, at the small, brick caretaker's cottage, the green lawns, the gardens. It was all so overwhelming.

He brought the car to a stop before the front door. ''It's not going to be so bad, you know,'' he said as he turned off the engine and shifted to look at her. "I'll be on my best behavior. I promise."

He was irresistible, and she had to smile. "I'll hold you to that," she said. "Now, where do I go?"

The butler had appeared on the steps. Cam waved toward him, looking suddenly distracted.

"I just remembered a phone call I was supposed to make to New York about an hour ago. These time changes are always messing me up. I'll let Maxwell take care of you."

He got out and took her cases from the trunk, dropping them on the front steps.

"I'll be by in a bit to see how you've settled in."

"Oh, don't bother," she called after him, but he was already taking the steps two at a time, obviously anxious to get to the telephone.

She turned to smile at Maxwell, who was fixing her with a wary eye. "Where to?" she asked.

"This way." He turned and started off down the driveway instead of going on into the house, and he didn't offer to help carry her cases.

She grinned as she bent to pick them up herself. This was the difference, she supposed, between being a guest and being a worker. But she didn't mind. She would just as soon have that demarcation clearly delineated.

Trudging behind him, she looked about at the rolling green lawns, the white fence, the background of snowcapped mountains. What a wonderful place to live in. Despite everything else, she was going to enjoy the scenery.

"Here we are." Maxwell turned and glared at her.

The servants' wing. But of course. Just where she belonged.

"In here?" she asked, looking in toward a dark little door hidden under the stairwell.

"This is the room Madam has assigned you. If you have any complaints, take them up with her."

"Oh, I won't have any complaints," she assured him hastily. "This will be fine."

And if it were too bad, say full of spiders and dripping faucets, she would just go home.

She smiled at him, amused by his studied animosity. "Thank you." She stuck out her hand, just to surprise him. "I hope we'll be friends. We'll be working together all summer, you know."

He stared at her hand with a ferocious scowl and when he finally took it, his fingertips barely touched her skin, and he withdrew them again.

"We'll see about that," he muttered. "Oh, here's the key."

He handed her a small, dark piece of metal and turned to shuffle back toward the main section of the house.

Ann shook her head and grinned, then scrunched in under the stairwell to open the door and survey her new abode. It was small. It was cramped. But it was also clean and would do quite nicely. She slung her cases on the bed and began to unpack.

She heard Cam's steps on the gravel outside just before he flung open the door and bellowed, "What the hell is this?"

She blinked at him, startled.

"Whose idea is this?" he demanded, his face dark with anger. "No way. Absolutely no way."

Surging into the room, he began throwing her things back into her bag.

"What are you doing?" She would have tried to stop him but there was something almost scary about the anger she saw in him. She stood back and watched instead.

"You're coming with me," he ordered, taking both cases under one arm and taking her hand with the other. "This place isn't fit for a dog."

"No, really, Cam, I like it," she protested rather ineffectually as she let him pull her toward the main house.

"I don't."

"But, Cam." She tugged on his arm and finally got him to stop and listen for a moment.

"Will you hear me out? The servants' wing will be fine. That's exactly what I am, and exactly where I belong."

His blue eyes were stormy and his features were frozen hard. "No, it's not. You're not a servant, Ann. You're a friend. A very old friend. A very important part of my past."

She didn't know what to say to that and his face softened. His fingers tightened on her hand.

"You're not some stranger who's been hired to do a job and then disappear. You're part of the fabric that makes me what I am." His sudden smile was bittersweet. "Who knows? I just may need you to help me save my soul some day."

Ann was speechless and a feeling of dread was growing in her chest. Still, when he turned and started toward the house again, she came along willingly enough. When he presented his case in such emotional terms, she wasn't sure what else she could do.

They went through the side door into the library, out into the hall and through to the front stairway, then mounted the steps. At the top, Cam turned right and opened the door to a beautiful room with a large bay window overlooking the pool, the putting green and the meadows that led into the foothills and the mountains beyond.

The room itself had a huge canopied bed and lovely antique dressers, dressing table and wardrobes.

"Oh, Cam," Ann said, turning to look at the room. "Oh, this is too...too..."

"It's not 'too' anything. It's just right." His face had a stubborn look. "It's where I want you." He put her suitcases on the valet. "And now I'm going to find out why my mother put you out in no man's land."

"Cam, don't. Leave it alone."

But he was already heading into the hallway. Ann didn't want a rancorous argument on her very first day here. Cam's temper seemed short. There was no telling what he might say. She hurried along behind him to see if she could help defuse the situation.

"Mother?" he called, going down the stairs.

There was no answer, no sign of life. He stood in the middle of the parlor and looked around, a frown on his face. He hardly seemed to notice that Ann was following him.

"Ah-hah." He cocked an accusatory finger toward the solarium and started toward the door.

"Cam," Ann said, hurrying behind him. "Your mother had a right to put me anywhere she wanted me, and I really don't want to mess up my relationship with her."

He flung open the door to the solarium and there was Mrs. Sterling at the far windows, leaning against the glass and looking out.

"Oh my," she said, jumping as they entered.

Cam glared at his mother, then outside. "Mother, this is an outrage. You've given Ann the smallest, darkest, dirtiest room in the servants' quarters. I think you owe her an apology."

"Oh dear." Mrs. Sterling looked flustered. "Oh, I am sorry. I certainly didn't mean for that to happen. I'll see that another room is prepared for you immediately."

Ann opened her mouth but Cam spoke before she could get a word out.

"Never mind. I've already seen to it."

"Good. I assure you, Ann, I didn't realize we even had a room so awful. I hope you'll be happy in your new room. Please let Maxwell know if there is any problem. But most of the servants seem quite pleased with the accommodations at the—"

"I didn't leave her out there," Cam told her sternly. "In fact, I brought her into the main house. Ann is not a servant, Mother. I want to make that perfectly clear to you. Ann is a friend who is doing us a favor taking this job. We owe her a lot. As far as I'm concerned, she's a guest in our home. I hope you'll treat her that way, too."

Ann flushed, wishing he wouldn't make such a point of it. But Mrs. Sterling didn't seem to take umbrage. She nodded and smiled.

"Of course," she said quite pleasantly. "I'm quite sorry, Ann. I hadn't thought this through." She turned back to Cam. "What room have you given her?" she asked with friendly interest.

Cam hesitated a beat too long. "I put her in the Green Room," he said at last, rather defensively.

Mrs. Sterling's eyes widened and she looked quickly from Cam to Ann. "Oh," she said knowingly. "I see."

"No, you don't see at all," Cam continued stiffly. "I just . . . want her there. That's all."

"Of course." Mrs. Sterling began to walk toward the exit. "It's a very nice room. I'm sure she'll like it." She reached the doorway and looked back. "And it will be so convenient, with the connecting door to your room and all." And then she was gone and there was only a soft whisper as the door closed behind her.

"What?" Ann demanded, whirling to glare at Cam. "What connecting door?"

He had the grace to look at least a little bit sheepish. "Oh, it's nothing. Just an old door that hasn't been opened in years and years." He smiled and shrugged. "Pay it no mind. Ignore it. Pretend it doesn't exist."

"Cam. . . ."

"Listen, it might as well not exist. You didn't even notice it, did you? And I won't ever use it. I promise."

She sighed, looking at him with exasperation. "Why do you suppose I'm not getting that overwhelming rush of confidence those words should inspire?"

"Come on, Ann. Trust me."

"Trust you? What exactly have you done to inspire trust? I'm supposed to risk...having my peace of mind disturbed just because you tell me to trust you?"

His face took on a stubborn look. "Well, look at what *I'll* be risking. After all, you could come crashing into my room some night. All it might take would be one bad dream or one thunderstorm, and the next thing I would know, I might have some woman creeping into my bed. Disturbing my sleep. Messing up my covers." His sigh sounded more like longing than despair. "What a thing to have to worry about, night after night."

She rolled her eyes and turned away, and he came after her.

"Come on, Ann. I really won't bother you. And I want you to have that room. You deserve it."

She heard the sincerity in his tone, saw it in his eyes. Slowly, reluctantly, she nodded.

"All right, Cam. I'll stay there." She raised a finger in warning. "But you just trespass on my privacy once and I'll be out of there so fast..."

He put up a hand like a scout taking an oath. "I won't. You just wait and see how trustworthy I am."

She was tired. All she wanted to do was unpack and lie down for a quick nap. Her shoulders sagged wearily. "Okay. Okay." She glanced at her watch. "Time is fleeting, and I have things to do. I'll see you a bit later."

She left him behind and ran back up the stairs, her hand sliding along the silky smooth wood of the polished banister. What a place this was. And what a summer she was in for.

Four

To her surprise, Ann had a much better time than she'd expected the rest of the day. The staff, whom she made a point of meeting, was for the most part cooperative and friendly. She did envision having problems with Maxwell. He was a crusty old curmudgeon, but she was determined not to let him get in her way.

That night she took dinner with the family at the long table in the dining room. Mrs. Sterling had invited friends to the meal, an elderly couple who were both hard of hearing and tended to shout up and down the table. Cam egged them on, shouting right back, which delighted the guests but seemed to wear Mrs. Sterling's nerves to a frazzle, until in desperation, she waved away dessert and took her guests out onto the veranda.

"Was it something I said?" Cam asked innocently.

"You're impossible," Ann informed him, wiping her lips and laying down her napkin. "Now, if you will excuse me..."

"No." He was shaking his head, his face serious. "Sorry. Can't do that."

"Oh really?" She stared at him. "Why not?"

"We've got to talk."

He rose, carrying his coffee cup with him, and sank into a chair by her side. "We've got business, you and me. So let's get into it."

"Business?" she asked warily, leaning back in her chair. Why was it that she never trusted his motives? She was afraid it might have something to do with the way she reacted to his physical presence. She only hoped he couldn't read the signs of her discomfort. She could just imagine his wicked grin if he caught on to just how much he disturbed her.

But he seemed all seriousness now, his mind on other things.

"Sure," he said. "The parties. Isn't that what you're here for?"

"Well, yes, but your mother..."

"My mother's plans for parties are all very well, but since these things are being given in my name, I think I should have some say in the themes. I've been giving the matter some thought, and I've come up with a few ideas."

Sitting back in her chair, she couldn't help but smile at him. "Okay," she said. "Shoot."

He blinked. "As in a Western theme?"

She frowned. "No. No, I wasn't talking about... Oh, Cam, just tell it to me straight."

"Right." He gave her a small salute. "Here's my plan. How about we do away with themes altogether? Themes are for kids. I'm a mature adult, and I hope the woman I marry will be the same. What do we need with all this playacting?"

Ann smiled. "Your mother seems to like themes."

"I know. She always has. When I was young, my birthday parties usually looked like the circus had come to town. Half the time I would be gone, up in the hills with my old dog Trudy and a fishing pole, and everyone else would be back here playing clown and trapeze artist."

The thought of him trudging off with a fishing pole over his shoulder made a delightful picture. She had to stifle a grin at the scene that came to mind.

"Have you talked to your mother about dropping the themes?"

He made a face which she read as either yes, until he was blue in the face and she wouldn't listen, or no, he didn't dare, because he knew what the result would be.

Ann smiled again. "I think you're stuck with the themes," she said gently. "These parties are her idea."

He sighed. "Marrying me off is her idea, too," he grumbled.

That was a subject Ann wasn't about to get into. "Let's go with the themes, at least for the first party, and if it turns out to be horrible, we'll see if we can't negotiate for something else," she suggested.

"Oh, all right." He took a long sip of coffee. "But if we must have the themes, they ought to at least be imaginative. Not the same old things."

"Tell you what." Ann rose, laying down her napkin. She could sense a long evening coming if she didn't do something to head it off. "I've got a meeting at nine in the morning with your mother and Maxwell, to go over exactly this subject. Why don't you join us?"

He looked up at her, his eyes veiled. "Maybe I'll do that," he said softly. Reaching out, he circled her wrist with his fingers. "I want you to be comfortable here, Ann," he said. "Treat this house as your own. And let me know if anything at all bothers you." His fingers tightened and his gaze darkened. "One of these nights we have to have a long talk."

A tremor of alarm shivered through her, but she smiled and nodded and pulled away. A long talk could have only one subject that she could think of—Johnny. And that was something she didn't want to get into with him.

He didn't do another thing to stop her from leaving, much to her surprise. She escaped up to her room, took a long bath, but the subject kept nagging at her. Johnny. She knew it was inevitable that they bring it all out into the open at some time. And she knew she should welcome that. So why did she feel so hesitant?

Johnny and Cam had become so close that year. They had done almost everything together. She knew they had spent long Saturday afternoons playing basketball and then lying around Cam's pool, talking about their dreams, their aspirations. Johnny had told her about it many times.

And then Cam had left for the East Coast. Nothing had been said about getting together again, but Johnny had assumed Cam would be back at some time, Thanksgiving or Christmas, and that they would get together.

But Mr. Sterling had died around that time, and Mrs. Sterling had gone East, too, to stay with relatives for a few years and get over her loss. So Cam didn't come back for a long time. And he didn't call or write.

Ann and Johnny continued to date and became closer and closer. He was busy with the family grocery store. Bit by bit, Cam was pretty much forgotten, a footnote to their high school years. Johnny's father died and Ann and Johnny had a quick, quiet wedding. And then began the long struggle to keep the store afloat.

That store meant everything to Johnny. His grandfather had started it sixty years before, and his father had run it with tender loving care for a long time. When Johnny finally inherited it, everything seemed to go wrong. A huge new market opened in town, with video rentals and a salad bar. Progress was passing the corner neighborhood store by. Bit by bit, the store began to fail.

Johnny knew he needed to modernize, but by that time he didn't have the capital. Banks turned down his requests for loans, or asked such high-interest rates, he didn't see how they could swing it. Finally, Ann had had the idea of writing to Cam.

He was famous by then. Every move he made was being charted by the national media. It was common knowledge that he was very rich in his own right.

Johnny had resisted writing, but Ann had kept after him. And finally, against his better judgment, he'd sent Cam a letter. The form letter rejecting his request had come just a few days later. Cam's signature had looked hard and insolent. Johnny had been crushed.

And Ann had realized that the secret crush she had carried around for years had been directed toward a man who had turned into a cold, unfeeling entrepreneur.

That hardly seemed to jibe with the Cam she knew now. Still, she had the reply in her desk drawer at home. Johnny had reached out to Cam in his hour of need, and Cam had slammed the door shut in his face.

The store went under. And Johnny died. And that was the end of the story.

And now, here was Ann, in the lion's den, snuggled under the thick comforters of a huge, canopied bed. Living in luxury. This was it, wasn't it? She only hoped she didn't get so used to this she wouldn't be able to go back to her own little house and live like a normal person again.

In the morning she rose early and picked up a sweet roll and orange juice in the breakfast room and took them with her as she strolled about the grounds, looking in on the horses, finding the diamond drops of dew in the flower garden, listening to the birds sing in the trees. Even the air seemed more special here.

"Same old air," she chided herself. "Same old weather. Same old dirt beneath my feet."

But it wasn't the same, and she knew it. Would she still be the same when this summer was over?

She was in the library, waiting, when the others arrived a little after nine. She had her notebook and her pen in hand, looking very efficient with her glasses on her nose and her hair tied back neatly. Mrs. Sterling, who smiled at her, was followed by Maxwell, bringing in the menu planners.

Then Cam walked in. He wore a white shirt and designer jeans and looked younger than his years. His gaze quickly swept the room, lingering on Ann for a moment before he smiled.

"Good morning, everyone," he said in his best boardroom voice. "Shall we get right down to work?"

Maxwell made a grumpy sound and Mrs. Sterling fluttered like a bird, but no one challenged his right to chair the meeting. He sat down, the morning light coming in through the high library windows glistening in his hair like a shower of gold.

"Themes," he said, looking from one face to another. "Do we really need them?"

Mrs. Sterling went pale, her mouth slack with surprise. She looked about helplessly, her fingers playing with the hem on her jacket. "Oh, I . . . I . . ."

A bit to her own surprise, Ann jumped in, feeling sorry for her.

"Themes are very important to parties like this," she said quickly. "You're going to be mixing a lot of people who don't necessarily know each other. Themes give them something to talk about, something of a common denominator to move from. They feel more secure because they've been told exactly what is expected of them. I think it would be a mistake to dispense with the theme motif for the first party, at least. I say we go ahead for now and have an evaluation of how it worked after the party is over."

She stopped to catch her breath and looked about at the others. Maxwell was glaring at her as though he had a hangover and her voice had activated it. Mrs. Sterling was looking at her with grateful surprise. And Cam was laughing.

"Et tu, Brute?" he asked in a stage whisper.

"I'm only saying what I think," she responded smartly.

He pretended to frown. "Are you aware of the theory that women shouldn't be allowed to think at all?" he asked. "But no, I certainly don't want to arouse your feminist instincts," he added quickly. "So we'll forget about that. And we'll go with the theme business, at least for the first party. The question remains, what should that first theme be?"

Everyone seemed to have an idea, from Oriental Fantasies to Mrs. Sterling's favorite clowns with balloons that she had clung to since Cam's childhood. Cam vetoed everything he heard, especially the clowns.

"Well, then, let's hear your ideas," Ann prodded.

He brightened. "I've got some super ideas. How about a Great Gatsby theme? I could just wander around in a white suit and look rich and women could be instructed to throw themselves before me."

Ann shook her head. "Too sexist," she murmured.

"Okay." He hunched forward, getting into it. "Now here is my best idea ever. We could have the whole place turned into a striptease club. The women could just come in one by one and strip for me. I could have a scorecard that we illuminate on a monitor—"

"Cam!" Mrs. Sterling and Ann both said it at the same time.

He looked from one to the other, his face radiating innocence. "What? You people just can't face reality. Let's get down to bare essentials here. What we're setting up is a meat market. Why try to hide it?"

Ann was having a hard time keeping up with his fluctuations. One moment his words seemed to be full of casual humor, the next, they were dripping with something very close to bitterness. She could understand that he was uncomfortable with the whole concept of this search for a mate, but he had made a bargain with his mother and he would have to stick with it.

She found herself surprisingly protective of Mrs. Sterling. She liked the woman and she wasn't sure why. She knew Cam loved his mother dearly and wouldn't hurt her for the world. So why did he say these things? Why did he let his tongue grow sharp and cutting when he didn't need to?

She threw Cam a glance full of remonstration and said, "What we are setting up here is an old-fashioned coming out party. Only you are the one coming out. So mind your manners. Etiquette is an important part of the process."

An appreciative glint appeared in his blue eyes.

"Okay, okay. I'll be good. Themes. Well then, how's this? A Hawaiian luau, like they used to have in the fifties and early sixties."

He seemed to be talking directly to her, so she responded. "How do you know what they used to have in the fifties?"

He grinned knowingly. "I've watched a bit of television in my time. I've see the reruns. We could rent all the old beach party movies and take a look."

She still wasn't sure if he were serious or just setting up another joke.

"I suppose you want all the woman in hula skirts?"

"Sarongs, honey." His eyes took on a dreamy look. "No, wait a minute. How about bikinis?"

Ann and Mrs. Sterling exchanged glances and didn't say a word.

"The decorations would be easy," Cam went on. "Lots of palm fronds. We could roast a pig in a hole in the ground."

There was a strangling noise from Maxwell, but he ignored it, going on with growing enthusiasm.

"Luaus are great. There are dancing girls, flowers, lomilomi salmon, poi..."

In the end, the luau idea fit in best with the ideas that Mrs. Sterling had already explored. They went with it.

The meeting broke up and Ann left quickly, not giving Cam a chance to pull her aside for any more of his provocative teasing. The date was two weeks down the line and there was a lot to do.

In fact, the work load proved to be time-consuming but a lot more fun than she'd expected. Little by little, Mrs. Sterling came to depend on her for more than just the food. Auditioning Hawaiian dancers, choosing muumuu material, hiring flame-eaters and ukelele players, all suddenly became part of her responsibility, and she found herself rushing from place to place, delving into topics caterers seldom cover.

In the meantime, Mrs. Sterling was busy every day with candidates for Cam's affections. A stream of beautiful young women flowed through the Sterling premises, some staying for a night or two, some just for the afternoon. The lucky ones got to play tennis with Cam, or go for a horseback ride at daybreak, or an afternoon swim.

Ann managed to pretty well ignore these sessions. She was much too busy to let them bother her.

Another thing that surprised her was how busy Cam seemed to be. He was on the telephone to New York for hours every day, and the rest of the time was taken up by the candidates. She'd thought that she would be seeing a lot more of him than she did.

At night when she went to bed, sometimes she could hear him moving about in his room. One night she could have sworn he was doing jumping jacks, and she had to bite on the corner of her pillow to keep from laughing out loud.

But she got up early for breakfast and was usually out and working before he awoke. In the evening she liked to borrow one of the cars and run home to water her plants and check on her house. As often as not, she would grab a hamburger or fix herself some soup there rather than eat the more formal dinner at the Sterling house.

She'd been there a little over a week when one evening, after staying awake late to finish a mystery she was reading, she got an overwhelming craving for a midnight snack. She knew the staff would be long gone and she thought she'd heard Cam come in hours ago. Why not?

There was a full moon so light streamed in from various windows, making her journey through the huge house less of a problem than it might have been. She padded softly on bare feet, finding her way to the kitchen.

The room was cold and bare, the shapes eerie from the shadows the muted light produced. She shivered and reached quickly to open the refrigerator, letting that light fill the room in its comforting way.

There was plenty of bread and a wonderful prime rib that had barely been touched. She made herself a sandwich and started back through the house, carrying it away on a paper plate.

She was coming through the living room when a sound made her freeze. Someone was trying to get in the front door.

She stood very still, heart beating, and watched as the knob turned in the moonlight. She jumped as the door flew open, then sagged with relief when it was Cam who stepped inside.

He saw her immediately. "Hi," he said. "Fancy meeting you here."

She took in a deep breath to make up for the air she'd lost. "Where have you been?"

He looked at her strangely and she thought, "Oh, my gosh. He's been out with a woman. And it's certainly none of my business."

"Scratch that question," she said quickly. "You're a big boy. I guess you don't need to tell anyone where you've been, do you?"

He shrugged. "I don't mind telling you where I've been," he said calmly. "I tried to go to bed. But something kept me awake. It must be the full moon." He glanced at the sandwich in her hand. "You, too?"

"I was reading late. I just got the urge for a snack."

He nodded. "I went down to that little country and western bar down on Oklahoma Street. Do you know it?"

"I think I do."

"They've got a singer there this week—Bobby Garner. Maybe you've heard of him. I used to know him years ago. He sang backup to Dusty Autumn."

"That country singer who's so big?"

He nodded, looking at her, his mood somehow melancholy. "Come talk to me. I don't want to go to bed. Do you? No. You've got a whole sandwich in your hand. Come on back to the kitchen and we'll eat sandwiches together."

It was against her better judgment. Everything seemed to be against her better judgment where Cam was concerned. But she went along with him, glad that he turned on the light in the kitchen before he began to rummage through the refrigerator.

He chose ham and Swiss rather than the prime rib, and poured them both large glasses of milk. Sitting down beside her at the long table, he began to eat. But his first question came out of left field, throwing her off again.

"Are there some nights when you just miss Johnny more than others?" he asked softly.

Startled, she turned so that she wouldn't have to look him in the face. Her heart was beating very hard again.

"I always miss Johnny," she said simply. "But it's not like a knife in my heart anymore."

He was quiet for a moment, and then spoke again. "Would you say you're over him?"

She hated this, hated talking about Johnny this way. There was so much unfinished business between Johnny and Cam, business that would never be resolved. What good did it do to stir the embers this way?

"I'll never be over him," she said shortly.

"No, I know that. I don't mean that you've ripped him out of your heart. But are you beyond the place where every time you are out in a crowd, you expect to see him coming at you all of a sudden? Where every time you think of something funny, you want to go tell him? Are you beyond that?"

This wasn't pleasant. He was reminding her of pain she would just as soon forget.

"Yes," she said shortly. "I've been beyond that for years."

He was quiet again, and suddenly she realized what his questions meant. He had felt the same way at some time in his life about somebody. He wouldn't have phrased the questions that way if he hadn't.

Cam Sterling with a heart capable of being broken. It was a novel concept.

He was still quiet, drinking his milk and staring at the stove. Because of the things he had been saying, Ann was at a loss as to how she might get the conversation going. She didn't want to talk about Johnny. Someday she was going to have to ask Cam why he'd hurt him, and then she would have to explain how she could never forgive him for what he had done. But the time wasn't right for that.

"I thought I was in love, once," Cam was saying softly. "It was ten years ago. Her name . . . was Dusty Autumn."

So that was it. "The singer?"

He nodded. "She wasn't famous then. She just wanted to be."

Ann had no idea if she was supposed to ask for more information or not, and she let it lie, letting him decide for himself which way the flow of the conversation would go. So she had only herself to blame when he brought it right back to where she didn't want it.

"Tell me about Johnny. What did he do after I left?"

She stiffened, then forced herself to relax. After all, it was only fitting that he show some concern for what had happened to Johnny. It was also about time.

"He went to work in his father's store."

"I remember that store. We used to go down there and torment Mr. Dupree until he paid us off with apples or a candy bar, just to get rid of us."

She heard the warmth in his voice as he went over the memories and she looked at him curiously, searching his face. Maybe he really had loved those days. Maybe he really had meant to be a friend to Johnny. But how could she possibly tell for sure at this late date?

"When did you two get married?" he asked as he polished off his sandwich.

"Right after I graduated from high school."

"You didn't want to go to college?"

She hesitated. It had been so long since she'd thought about those days. "Actually, I had a scholarship to the University of the Sierras. But Johnny needed me. So..."

He stopped, staring at her. "You gave up college because he needed you?"

Why did he think that so strange? Maybe people in his milieu didn't sacrifice for love. "Sure."

He was staring at her, making her feel extremely uncomfortable. She was aware of the blond hair on his forearm, so close to her now as he let his arm lie on the table beside her. Why was she here with this man in the middle of the night? It didn't make a lot of sense.

"No one has ever done anything like that for me," he said softly at last.

"The question is, have you ever done anything like that for anyone else?" she returned quickly, not willing to let him get maudlin.

He looked at her for a moment, then laughed, reaching out to touch her hair at the same time.

"Ann, you would be so good for me," he said lightly. "I've got to find a woman like you to marry— someone who will keep me on my toes and make sure I don't take myself too seriously."

She looked away, brushing crumbs into a pile on the table.

He went on, his voice very quiet in the night air. "You know, Ann. You hear all the time about men going into midlife crisis."

She glanced at him. "You're hardly middle-aged."

"I feel old sometimes. I've done a lot. I've been a huge success in business. There's no place I could say I would want to do anything differently. And yet...as a person, as a human being, I'm not so sure that I've done the right things with my life. I wish there was some way you could find out, some objective measure to use..."

He gazed into her eyes, the smile slowly fading from his, and she gazed back. His fingers began to sink into her hair, his hand drawing her nearer. And as though she had no choice, she moved closer.

It could have been the night air, the full moon, the warm comfort of a man's arms around her. She didn't know, couldn't even begin to guess. But his kiss intoxicated her, sent her spinning into that special place where nothing mattered but scent and touch and the sound of breathing.

Tonight he was gentle, his kiss a question, a tantalizing suggestion of things to come. She didn't give him an answer, but she didn't turn him away, either, and the longer the kiss lasted, the further from reality she floated.

He was so large, so warm, so strong, and instinctively she craved the feel of his body against hers. And so she let the kiss go on, and then her arms were around his neck so that she could press closer, her breasts rising hard against him. She wanted to feel the muscles of his hard chest, the bulge of his bicep against her shoulder. Excitement surged through her. She wanted him.

This didn't mean a thing, couldn't mean a thing, mustn't mean a thing, and yet, she couldn't stop. There was something in her taking over, opening to him as though she needed him too badly to let go.

With Johnny, lovemaking had always been a conscious thing. She'd loved Johnny dearly and relations between them had been great. But never like this.

With Cam it seemed almost to be a fever in her blood. With Cam, it could become an obsession.

It wasn't fair, not to Johnny, not to her. He was the good one. He was the one who had deserved the best she had to offer. Not Cam, not this playboy who had turned his back on them all for so long.

She pulled away from Cam, dismayed with him, dismayed with herself. How could she betray Johnny this way? And with the very man who had hurt him most.

"Ann?" His voice was husky with desire. "Ann, I would never hurt you—"

"Don't make promises you can't keep, Cam," she interrupted sharply, pulling herself back together and rising from her seat.

"I never do that, Ann."

She turned and glared down at him, her own guilt fueling her anger. "Oh really? Tell that to Johnny, why don't you?"

And then she was gone, moving through the dark house like a shadow, escaping to her own room.

Five

Okay, first off, the kiss had been a mistake. He'd decided that first day he had moved Ann into the bedroom next to his that there would be no kissing and, most certainly, no sex.

It wasn't that he wasn't attracted to her. Not at all. In fact, he was too damn attracted for his own good. The way his pulse jumped whenever he looked at Ann was shaking his hold on his senses, making him lose sight of the objective.

Cam turned his horse out across the meadow, toward the foothills, and rode hard, the pounding of the hooves on the loam keeping time to the racing of his thoughts.

She was a friend. And that was the way she would have to stay. That was ordained by the history they shared.

And what was that history? He hated to bring this up, even in his own mind. But he had to face reality.

That history was Johnny. Pure and simple.

Johnny. He could remember him so clearly, laughing, eager, ready to go along with any crazy scheme Cam might think up. Ready to listen to secrets. Ready to sympathize with losses. Ready to share anything he had, anything he felt.

But not Ann. He wouldn't have shared Ann. And now when Cam went back in his mind to that night of the senior picnic, he knew why he had walked away from Ann, even though that kiss had been so disturbing.

The guys had kidded Johnny for weeks about not having a girl. He'd reddened every time and mumbled something about not having enough time for dates. Friday nights he always claimed he had to work, a claim that had puzzled Cam when he'd dropped by the store and found only Mr. Dupree tending the counter.

Johnny had been out with Ann, of course. But he hadn't wanted anyone to know about it. Johnny had known how special Ann was, and he'd kept that secret to himself.

Instinctively Cam knew why. Johnny wouldn't want to talk about her the way the other guys talked about the girls they went out with. It would have killed Johnny to have them ask how far he'd gotten with her, to have insisted on details. For all his happy-go-lucky nature, Johnny had been blessed with a streak of stubborn pride that would have turned him to stone before he would have divulged anything about the girl he loved.

Even to Cam.

The night of the senior prom, all secrets were revealed. Funny that he didn't remember Ann from that night. But he did remember that Johnny had admitted at last that he had a girlfriend. And they'd all razzed him, good-naturedly.

The next night had been the picnic. He remembered how Johnny had left with some of the others to get drinks, and how he'd said, "Take care of my girl for me," to Cam, and only to Cam. It was Cam he trusted.

And it was Cam who had betrayed him.

He reined in his horse and let him walk along the banks of the sludgy river, hardly seeing the cattails or the opposite fields of alfalfa. He was back seventeen years, living it again.

He hadn't thought twice about kissing Ann that night. He'd been on a natural high, hugging and kissing every girl who offered him a chance. So when he'd turned and taken Johnny's girl into his arms, he hadn't done it with the intent of stealing anything from him.

But that kiss had been unlike any he'd ever had. By the time he'd pulled away, he'd been changed, and he knew it.

He also knew he'd taken something that didn't belong to him. He'd trespassed on forbidden territory. And he'd backed away very fast.

Ann was Johnny's girl. Then and now. The kissing had to stop.

And as for that thing she had said—"Tell that to Johnny..." implying he didn't know how to keep promises—what the hell had she meant by that?

True, he had walked away from everyone here and never looked back. There had always seemed time, time to get back to old friends, time to make up for forgetting.

But time had turned on him. Time had swallowed up Johnny. Time had robbed him of the best friend he'd ever had.

No.

He grimaced, angry with himself. That was a copout. Time hadn't done a thing to him. He'd done it to himself. He could have written, picked up the phone, even run by to see Johnny on one of his infrequent visits home when he had begun coming back to California again. And he never had. He'd never made the effort.

Was that what Ann was referring to? Or was there some other promise she knew about that he didn't remember? It made his head hurt just to try puzzling it out and he gave up, kneeing his horse into a gallop again and riding hell for leather across the meadow.

It was too late to find Johnny. But it wasn't too late to take care of his girl. And that was what he meant to do.

Here it was. Doomsday.

It was late afternoon and the luau was at hand. Ann's nerves were making her jump out of her skin at the tiniest noises.

Was she ready? Where were the orchids? Half of the Hawaiian muumuus had arrived in childrens' sizes and had to be rushed back and replaced. The singer who had sworn up and down he could warble a great "Hawaiian Wedding Song" had come down with chicken

pox and the band had brought along a comic enter-
tainer instead—a man who wanted to wear a coconut
bra and throw rubber chickens at the audience. She'd
sent him packing.

But the problems hadn't stopped there. Overnight,
black algae had invaded the swimming pool and birds
had decimated the newly planted poppies.

"Disaster city," Ann kept muttering to herself as
she raced from one crisis to another. Oh well, if she
was fired, at least she could go back to her little house
and live in peace.

She was in the kitchen checking on last-minute
preparations for the food when Mrs. Sterling appeared. "Now, tell me, how are we coming along?"
she asked.

"Well—" Ann turned and gestured toward a large
pot on the counter "—here's the poi."

Mrs. Sterling stared at the awful-looking substance. "What does it taste like, exactly?"

Ann stifled a smile. "They often compare it to library paste, and I would have to agree with that as-
sessment."

"Are you kidding?" Cam had come in, injecting the
room with the usual excitement of his presence. "The
library paste we used to have in school when I was a
kid was great stuff. I used to eat it for protein instead
of peanut butter sandwiches. And this—" he scooped
up a fingerful and tried it, making a face "—is not
nearly as good. I guess it's an acquired taste."

"Are you going to wear that?" his mother asked
doubtfully, gazing at his jeans and shocking green T-
shirt emblazoned in bright pink with I Can't Help It.
It's In My Genes.

"Don't worry, Mother." He kissed her forehead with a loud smack. "I'll put on proper attire in due time."

His eyes met Ann's over his mother's head and she realized, with something of a jolt, that this was the first time they had really looked at one another since the night of the midnight snack. For days they seemed to have been studiously avoiding one another.

She regretted what she'd said that night. She knew she had hurt and puzzled him. She'd seen that in his eyes the moment the words had come out of her mouth. It had been a defensive gesture, a reflex against the way she could feel herself being pulled toward him. She'd had to protect herself. She still did.

What surprised her was he hadn't said a word to her about it since. He hadn't followed her then, and he still seemed to be avoiding the issue. He was generally such a straightforward type, she couldn't understand what was holding him back in this instance.

He'd been going around, avoiding her eyes, and saying hearty, prosaic things about what friends they were to anyone who would listen. He was obviously trying to manage emotions that were proving uncooperative.

They were going to have to talk this out. She was going to have to confront him with her resentments, and he would have to explain...

Explain? Was that what she was doing, hoping for an explanation? Something to make her feel less guilty, something to make it all right that she felt this compelling attraction every time she looked at him?

What a fool she was. When would she ever learn?

"Why don't you go on out and see about the pig?"
Mrs. Sterling was asking her son. "I can't do it. I can't
stand to look at the thing."

"All right," Cam answered, but he was still looking at Ann, and she was still looking back, wishing she
had the strength to frown at him, to let him know he
was nothing to her.

But there was no time for any of that. Before anyone could say another word, a new presence made itself felt in the kitchen. A tall, blond beauty burst
regally through the double doors and cried, "Dar-
lings! Here you both are!"

Mrs. Sterling started, then reached out in what
seemed to Ann to be excessive ecstasy. "Ursula!" she
cried in return. "Oh, Ursula, you are finally here!"

Cam came next to Ann. His bright eyes had taken
on the hunted look of a cornered stag. "Save me," he
whispered, clutching her arm. "Where can I hide?"

But his mother's opinion was obviously quite different. "Come in, come in, I want you to see everything, my dear." She rushed forward to greet the
woman. "Oh, Ursula. I've been telling your mother
almost daily that I needed you here. And you've finally come. You are going to stay with us for a while,
aren't you? Oh, stay for the summer, there's a good
girl. We really need you."

Ursula came into the room, an elegant, willowy
creature with huge violet eyes, looking everything a
perspective mother-in-law might want. She was wearing an expensive, stylish suit and had her hair piled in
a do that made her look over six feet tall. Marching
forward, she held her hand out to Cam.

"Cameron, darling," she cooed. "My soul mate." She presented her cheek and he kissed it dutifully. She straightened again and frowned at his T-shirt. "Hardly suitable attire, I should think."

And then she noticed his life-support clutch on Ann's arm and her eyes widened.

Cam only held Ann more tightly. His mouth twisted into something that didn't look much like a smile. "It's a luau, Ursula. Lighten up."

The woman looked as though she'd smelled a foul odor but was too polite to mention it. She turned away from Cam and back to where she was more welcome.

"Now show me every inch of this kitchen," she ordered Mrs. Sterling. "I want to see exactly what you are doing here."

"Who is she?" Ann asked softly as Mrs. Sterling, chattering happily, led Ursula to the sinks on the far side of the room. It was insidious, the way she felt herself naturally melting against him, wanted to mold herself to the shape of his body. Her skin felt hot and alive where he touched her. When she turned her face toward him, she could feel his breath on her cheek. Her heart was racing, a light, shallow beat that signaled excitement.

Did he notice? She couldn't really tell. He was watching Ursula and sighing.

"You see before you Ursula, the bridal candidate from hell," he whispered. "I'm not kidding. I've got to get out of here."

She looked at him. He was serious—and seriously worried. This had to be his mother's prime choice. Ann could read the signs. Despite everything, she felt a touch of sympathy for him.

"Why don't you go on out and check on the roasted pig, as your mother asked?" she reminded him.

"Good idea." He gave her arm a squeeze and started toward the door. "I'm gone," she heard him mutter as he disappeared.

Her arm, her whole side felt chilled with him absent. She rubbed the skin quickly, looking around to make sure no one had noticed how she swooned like a silent movie star whenever he touched her. It was ridiculous. And it surely had to stop.

She didn't have time to pay any more attention to Ursula. She had much too much to do. The red rice had to be molded, the lomilomi salmon steamed to perfection, the rice noodles soaked for the chicken long rice, and the small wooden bowls laid out for the poi.

She had molded banana leaves to wooden trays to use as serving bowls. There were vanda orchids to strew into the punch bowls and plumeria leis to hang from the lathework. The scent of flowers was everywhere, making her dizzy with the strong perfume. She could almost imagine they had been transplanted to the islands—until she heard the screech of brakes and the roar of four-wheel-drive tires on gravel, along with the high homey whine of genuine country music.

"Who on earth is that?" Mrs. Sterling muttered as she craned to look out the kitchen window.

They found out soon enough. Cam came into the kitchen moments later, followed by a tall, handsome man in cowboy boots and a bright aloha shirt.

"This is Bobby Garner, my old, old friend. Meet Ann Dupree, my even older friend." He grinned at her, his eyes shining with happy anticipation that made her wonder—was it because he was glad to have his friend here, or because he was looking forward to the party? She wasn't sure and she wasn't sure she even wanted to know the answer.

"Take good care of Bobby, won't you?" he said to her, touching her arm lightly, making it sizzle again. "I've got to run and change. People are beginning to arrive."

As if she didn't have two thousand and ten things to do herself. But looking at Bobby's open face, she could hardly refuse.

"I'm the caterer," she said. "And you must be the country singer."

He touched his finger to the brim of his hat. "You got that right. Cam invited me and I just had to come on out and see what one of these ritzy parties was like." His face changed. "Say, you look a little busy."

She nodded, feeling harried. "Listen, I hate to be rude to a friend of Cam's, but I'm afraid you've got your choice. Either go on over and sit on the veranda and wait for people to arrive, or take these straw hats and leis over to the pool house. That's where people are going to be asked to put on their Hawaiian costumes."

Her instincts had told her he would rather help than stand around, and she was right. Soon he was her right hand, and when it was all prepared, she knew she would never have made it on time without him.

The luau looked wonderful. An endless stream of limousines arrived, disgorging lovely women of all descriptions. A few had male escorts. Most came alone. The point, after all, was to provide Cam with as many women as his mother could gather to choose from.

It all seemed rather silly, and yet it was deadly serious to Mrs. Sterling. She kept drifting by Ann, muttering vague comments about bloodlines and antecedents and breeding, until Ann began to wonder if she'd got her son's prospective brides mixed up with the operations of her stud farm.

But once they had been dressed in the bright Hawaiian prints Mrs. Sterling had provided, the guests made a lovely picture around the swimming pool and under the arbor that had been constructed expressly for this party. The Hawaiian musicians played soft music, interspersed now and then with wilder sounds when the dancers came out and moved their hips to the drumbeats, waving feathered gourds and shouting Polynesian words, or when the heavily muscled Samoan dancers came out in abbreviated loincloths and whirled their swords or torches, acting macho and causing a small stampede toward the stage.

Cam was a constant presence. Every time she turned around, he was there, making a humorous comment, asking a question, giving her a quick hand with something, acting as though they were the best of friends, as though he needed her advice on every move he was about to make.

It was almost, she thought a bit resentfully at one point, as though it were the two of them against the world, and his choice of mate was supposed to be as important to her as it was to him.

She couldn't help but keep an eye on him as he made his way among the beauties who had assembled just for him. He was so tall, so handsome, and all the women seemed to bend and sway when he passed, like palm trees reacting to a breeze. All these women. Surely there would be one he would fall for.

Was that a twinge? She pressed her hand to her heart and bit her lip. No way. What Cam did with his life had nothing to do with her.

"Okay, what do you think of that one?" he asked her as she attempted to clear away some of the abandoned champagne glasses left on the grass. He took the glasses from her hand and gestured for her to turn around and take a look at his latest conquest.

Ann turned slowly. The girl waved, and she managed a three-fingered wave in return, feeling like an idiot. The prospect was short, redheaded, cute and pouty, with an hourglass figure that wouldn't quit. She also looked very young.

"Are you sure she's allowed to stay up this late?" Ann asked, knowing she was being catty and hardly caring at all.

But Cam didn't care, either. He seemed to enjoy her snippiness. "Hey, listen. I've got an open hunting permit on this whole herd. I can go all the way down to eighteen, no limit." He grinned. "So, what do you think?"

Ann wrenched the champagne glasses back out of his hand. She didn't want to glare at him. She knew it would look as though she were jealous if she did. But she couldn't help it. She glared anyway.

"I think you ought to ask your buddy for his opinion. Not me."

His face fell. "You're right," he said contritely. "She's too young." He sighed. "Oh well, back to the salt mines."

Ann watched as he led the girl back into the crowd and gracefully pawned her off on one of the few men present. A smile was tugging at her lips, and she hated herself for it. Then Cam stopped and began to talk to a raven-haired lovely in a pink sarong, and the smile evaporated again.

She turned away, determined to stop paying any attention to Cam or his courtship antics.

She didn't have time for that, anyway. She had too much on her mind. She had work to do, things to plan, crises to deal with.

And then there was Ursula.

Ursula seemed to have taken an unfortunate shine to Ann. She spent half her time hanging around, asking about Ann's work methods, and the other half chasing Cam from place to place.

"Are you planning to put on a luau yourself?" Ann asked her at last, exasperated by the flow of questions.

"Oh. Uh, no, not at all." She seemed a bit flustered by the thought. "I'm just curious, that's all." She looked at Ann for a moment and then seemed to decide she was worthy of a confidence.

"You do realize I'm the one, don't you?"

Ann looked at her blankly. "The one? What one?"

Ursula smiled a secretive, just-between-you-and-me smile.

"The one that Cam is going to marry. Oh yes. It was all settled years ago."

Ann didn't know where to look. She couldn't possibly keep a straight face if she stared the woman in the eyes. If she really thought Cam was going to marry her, she was in for a shock.

"Oh. Well. I . . . I wasn't aware . . ."

"All this party business is just a ruse. We've been betrothed since the day I was born. Our families have always been close. I've just been waiting for him to be ready."

Ann had no doubt Mrs. Sterling would have backed Ursula's view of reality to the hilt. But she wasn't so confident about Cam.

"Does Cam . . . know about this?" she asked delicately.

"Of course." She laughed softly. "He's a typical man. He loves to flirt with the ladies. But once I get him alone, we'll straighten this all out, and then Mrs. Sterling can forget about these silly parties."

Ann swallowed and looked away. She didn't adore Ursula, but it hardly seemed kind to let her live in this dreamworld. She had seen the look in Cam's eyes. He would sooner marry the upstairs maid than Ursula.

"Oh, there he goes now." Ursula had spotted Cam coming off the dance floor with the pink-saronged person. "I'd better go see if I can catch him. Just a little time alone to remind him of our commitments. That's all I need."

"Good luck," Ann whispered after her, shaking her head. Poor Ursula. She certainly foresaw disappointment in that woman's future.

But she had to get her mind back on her work. Things were running fairly smoothly. The food all made it to the table in time. The pig was carved. The dolphin-shaped ice sculpture arrived and sat in the middle of the serving table. After the disastrous beginning the day had skidded through, everything seemed to be running quite smoothly.

Ann took advantage of a lull to survey her accomplishment and deem it a success. This was the first time she had ever had this much to do with the planning and execution of such a lavish party. All in all, she thought she'd done a pretty good job.

"Got anything else I could do?"

She turned and smiled at Bobby Garner, who had come out to join her. "Not right now. You've been such a big help. Why don't you go on over and join the crowd? You deserve to have a little fun, too."

"I'll go." He held out a hand. "If you'll come, too. How about one dance?"

Ann felt her cheeks flush with surprise. "Oh . . . no. I couldn't. . . ."

He gave her a knowing wink. "Oh yes, you could."

And of course she did.

Her first impulse was to search out Cam in the crowd. He was dancing with Ursula and the moment she found him, he looked up and met her eyes.

"Damn," she muttered, looking away quickly and feeling cross. He would come over and offer to exchange partners any moment. She could feel it coming.

"Would you rather sit this one out?" Bobby asked.

"I . . . Do you mind if I just go back and get a drink of water?"

He went with her into the now-empty kitchen and leaned against the counter, looking back through the window at the bright splash of light that set off the party.

"This is really some shindig, isn't it? And all to get old Cam married off." He laughed. "Well, maybe he should have married Dusty back when he had the chance."

She finished the water in her glass and turned on the faucet to fill it again. Her heart was beating very quickly and she wasn't sure why.

"Did he...did he really have a chance?" she asked, trying to appear as casual as possible. "Were they that close?"

Bobby laughed out loud. "Sure, he'd have had a chance, if he'd hog-tied her fast enough. She was a go-getter, that girl. Anyone who wanted her would really have to go after her." He sobered, remembering. "I don't know. Maybe he just wasn't willing to put out the effort at the time. Maybe he wasn't that ready to get married."

That meant it was pretty serious, though. Ann was short of breath and she angrily cursed herself. It was so ridiculous to let herself get all choked up over some old girlfriend of Cam. Good Lord, the man was out there right now dancing with half the female population of California, and she was letting herself sink into agony over some old love from ten years ago?

"Do you think . . ." She could hardly get the words out. "If they got together now . . ."

"Him and Dusty? Naw. That's long gone. Dusty's got her sights on a higher glory now. She wants real fame. The kind that lasts forever. She wouldn't settle for any old human anymore."

It was shameful, this relief spilling through her. Utterly shameful. And utterly useless. Cam Sterling was not for her. Didn't she know that yet?

"Well, how about you?" she asked, managing to keep her newfound happiness under leash in her voice. "Weren't you her backup singer for a while? Why aren't you with her anymore?"

He looked at her and grinned, his good nature plain on his handsome face. "She dropped me like a lead balloon once fame began to come her way and she thought she just might hit the big time. Thought she needed someone with a little more polish, you know? I don't quite have that silk shirt look about me." He grinned. "I'm down-home and country, and that's all I ever want to be."

Ann smiled back at him. She liked Bobby Garner. A genuine person was rare in this day and age.

"Isn't that a coincidence, you having a singing engagement in town just when Cam came home for the summer?"

He wiggled his eyebrows at her. "Don't you tell anyone, Ann, because Cam didn't want me to spread it around, but that weren't no coincidence. Fact is, Cam got me the job."

That surprised her. "Really? When... I mean, how..."

"I was in New York a month or so ago, and I gave him a call. I'd been kind of down lately. My wife divorced me a year ago. She couldn't take all the moving around, you know? I could hardly blame her. But I hadn't been getting many gigs lately. You know, when you're down, the audience can just feel it, and they don't want to be entertained by anyone feeling worse than they do. They want some happiness. That's what they came for. Anyway, Cam could tell I wasn't exactly hittin' the high notes, and soon as he got out here in California, he gave me a call. Said he'd found a little club that needed a singer. Sent me a plane ticket. And here I am."

Ann didn't know what to say. What a generous gesture. How completely out of character. Unless . . .

Her mind was spinning toward all sorts of alternative explanations and she didn't want to deal with them right now. So she just smiled. "How nice of him," she said.

"Yup. And he's even invited me to move in here for a while. I'm thinking about taking him up on it."

"That would be great. We could use another face at the dinner table."

"I guess that Ursula person is staying here, too?"

Ann nodded. "So it seems."

"So, what's the deal between you and Cam?" he asked out of the blue, and the smile froze on her face.

"Wh-what do you mean? We're just friends."

"Just friends. Right. That's what he keeps saying, too. As a matter of fact, he said it so many times, that was what made me start to think that something was up. You know, the man who doth protest too much?"

She stared at him, struck by what he'd just said, struck by what she was feeling. Just friends. Just friends.

That was a lie. She knew it from the bottom of her heart. All this skirting around the issue for the last two weeks had been useless.

She was jealous when she saw him with other women. She felt faint when he touched her. She felt a glow of pride when she heard about him doing a good deed for someone. It was time she faced facts and learned how to deal with them.

She was crazy about Cam.

Six

The party was finally over.

The only vehicle left in the parking area was Bobby's, but he was just staying around to help Ann. Cam waved goodbye to the last limousine and turned back toward the house, lines of weariness etched on his face.

What a night. A merry little jog through hell couldn't have been more horrifying. It was almost enough to put a man off women permanently.

"Cameron. Where are you?"

Cam jumped at the sound of Ursula's voice and, coward that he was, quickly slipped through a side door into the garage. He couldn't take any more tonight. All he wanted to do was get into the hot tub and relax, soak all his tensions away.

But what was he thinking of? He wouldn't dare do that until he knew Ursula was in bed.

He groaned. Something told him she didn't sleep much. The prospect of sharing a hot tub with Ursula was downright daunting. The woman never stopped talking.

Well, how about a swim in the river? At least that promised to be more private.

"Oh, Cameron! Yoo hoo!"

No, she'd probably chase him down there, too. Cam leaned against the big old Rolls-Royce and closed his eyes. What had he done to deserve this? He'd always been a good son, sent birthday cards, never got arrested, not even for junk bonds. Why was his mother determined to torture him this way?

He heard the scratch, scratch, scratch of Ursula's high-heeled sandals skipping past and he waited, listening carefully for the all clear.

If he couldn't look forward to a soak in the hot tub, there was only one comforting experience left to explore. He felt himself relax even as he thought of it.

He would go find Ann. That was what he would do. A nice cup of coffee and a nice long talk with Ann. That would make him feel better.

He opened the side door to the garage and looked both ways. There was no sign of Ursula. Looking toward the kitchen, he noted the light still burning. Good. Ann was still there. There was nothing like a long, evening chat with a ... a friend. He started out across the grass, taking the shortcut.

Ann was exhausted. She'd been up since five that morning and she'd worked herself to a frazzle ever since. But the tired she felt was the good type, the one where success gave birth to satisfaction.

Sighing, she walked out into the yard and surveyed the pool area. The cleanup crew had done a good job. Only the trampled grass gave silent testimony to the party that had been in full swing just an hour before.

She heard someone coming from the area of the garage and she turned and saw Cam's body silhouetted against the light. He was coming straight toward her. Her pulse began to throb and she wrapped her arms tightly around her as though she'd felt a sudden chill.

The new feeling filled her, the new acknowledgement of how she felt about him, and she took a step in his direction, ready to meet him halfway.

"Oh! Cameron! There you are."

Ursula came out of the shadows, swooping like a bat, and pounced on him, scarves flying.

Caught by Ursula, he looked at Ann, his eyes those of a drowning man.

"Hi, Ursula," he said weakly.

"I've been looking for you everywhere. Cam, darling, I'm going to have to insist that you take me into town. I need to pick up some medicine to help me sleep." She pouted prettily, hanging on his arm. "You will take me, won't you?"

Cam looked at Ann again before he said, "Do you have to go tonight?" in a rather plaintive voice.

"Oh yes, yes, yes. I can't sleep if I don't have my medicine. And then you would have to sing me lullabies all night." She laughed as though she thought that quite a nice joke. Cam blanched and made a choking sound.

"You'd better take her," Ann said, though it galled her.

He looked at her and nodded sadly. "Let's go," he said to Ursula. "Let's get it over with."

He went off with his arm around Ursula's shoulders and Ann began to fume as she put away the last of the silver trays. Why was it that rich, beautiful women like Ursula always seemed to get their own way, no matter what?

Cam didn't like her, he didn't want her, and yet, she had that bulldog expression, that clear tenacity.

Ann stopped in her tracks, horrified by a thought. What if she pulled it off? Stranger things had happened. And people with intense determination and dogged persistence often got what they wanted out of sheer willpower. What if she actually did get him to marry her?

Suddenly a blast of country and western music split the night air, then the screech of tires on gravel, and finally, a woman's high-pitched shriek, sounding a lot like the screams one heard near a roller coaster.

She turned and there was Cam coming toward her with a big grin.

"What was that?" she asked, though she thought she knew.

"Ursula," he confirmed. "I got Bobby to take her."

"You didn't." Ann started to laugh. "How did you ever get her into his truck?"

"I practically had to bind her hands and feet. And then she saw Bobby. You heard the scream she let out?" He grinned happily. "He'll take real good care of her."

Their eyes met and Ann was suddenly almost shy, afraid he might read too much in her glance if she let him study it for too long. She turned and started back for the kitchen, knowing he would follow.

"Poor thing," she murmured.

"What do you mean, 'poor thing'? She's out to ruin my life, if I let her."

"Oh, she's not that bad." What was she saying? The woman was a menace. But there was something in the code of honor in the sisterhood that demanded she pretend to like her.

Cam had no such pretensions. "Not that bad? No, she's worse. The woman drives me crazy with her incessant talking. Half the time I'm not sure if she wants to romance me or sell me some life insurance."

She stopped at the sliding glass door and smiled at him teasingly. "I know why you don't like Ursula. She doesn't laugh at your jokes."

His eyes were warm as he looked back. "Laugh at my jokes? How could she? She never hears my jokes. She's too busy telling her own."

She ducked her head and slipped into the kitchen, walking slowly through the room. There was really nothing left to do, at least, nothing she wanted to tackle tonight. She walked on through to the den, strolling slowly.

The den was filled with photo albums and scrapbooks. There was a large one with Cam's name on it. She'd been eyeing it for days, waiting for a chance to take it down and look through it. Now, she noticed someone else had done just that. It was lying open on the window seat.

"Well, Cam," she said, running her finger over a sculpture of a cat's head that sat on a pedestal near the center of the room. "You've had about a hundred women here tonight, most every one of them just aching to take you home with her. You really had your choice."

She turned and looked at him, wondering if she dared ask the next question. "Did you find the girl of your dreams?" she asked softly at last.

She watched his eyes. Would there be a hint there? Would she know if he'd seen someone tonight he was interested in?

But all she could see was the quick flash of humor.

"How can I find the girl of my dreams when I'm living in a nightmare?" he asked her.

She laughed and he saw it, the new open feeling in her. It fascinated him, like a bright, shiny jewel, and his impulse was to reach for it, hold it in his hand, experience it.

He did reach for her hair. It had come partially loose from the bun she'd put it in that morning. He had only to pull out two pins and it fell like a shower of midnight around her shoulders, her perfume rising in a wave that sent his senses spinning. He breathed in slowly, watching her eyes.

She stared back, her head slightly tilted so that she could look up at him. His shirt was open, his tan skin warm and tantalizing. She'd never known another man who looked so good, felt so right. Could he tell? She couldn't hide it any longer, especially not from herself. She felt now as she had always felt. He was the only man who had ever reached this deeply into her soul.

"So you didn't choose a bride?" she asked softly.

His grin was slightly off center. "That just goes to show you what kind of an ornery cuss I am," he said. He touched her hair again, letting his fingers sift through it, his eyes darkening mysteriously. "My choice is always exactly what I can't have."

Her heart was beating so loudly she could hardly think, and the only thought that was going through her brain was, what made him think he couldn't have her?

But he was looking away, clearing his throat, and she watched, slightly puzzled, as he withdrew from her.

He was going. He was leaving her. She had to do something to keep him just a bit longer.

"Cam."

He turned back and looked at her questioningly.

She remembered the scrapbook in the window seat. "Look what's here." She went toward the scrapbook and looked back. He was coming to see what she'd found.

"Oh my God." A cynical smile hovered on his lips as he looked down at it. "So you've found the withered remnants of my celebrity."

His voice was dry, but when she sank down onto the window seat and took the scrapbook into her lap, he sat down beside her.

She turned pages, looking at headlines.

Boy Wonder Shakes Wall Street. Stock Whiz Sticks It To Competition. Young Broker Worth His Weight in Sterling.

And the pièce de résistance—the cover of a national magazine.

There he was looking young and proud and very arrogant.

"It must have been a wonderful time for you."

"It had its moments. The ups and the downs."

She looked sideways at him, her hair hanging like a curtain against her right cheek. "Do you miss it?"

"The celebrity stuff? Not a bit. I'm still pretty well-known in business circles, but I don't get mobbed in the produce section of the supermarket anymore."

He turned the page and looked at a picture of himself cutting a ribbon on a new building.

"That was spooky, having people swarm around you. You'd have thought I was a television game-show host or something, the way people came after me."

He shuddered, remembering. "They seemed to think they knew me. It was so odd. And just because they thought they knew me, I was supposed to treat them like friends. You know?" He grimaced. "I hated that."

He was sinking into the memories, remembering that hectic time. His eyes took on a glazed look as he went back.

"It was heady stuff. For a while, I actually had trouble remembering I wasn't really as great as everyone was saying I was."

She laughed softly. "You must have had something going for you."

"Luck. A little bit of talent and a lot of luck."

He was even modest. Ann stared down at the scrapbook without really seeing it any longer. What was happening to her? For years she had tried to hate Cam for what he'd done to Johnny. And now she was seeing only his good side. And that was all she wanted to see.

It was probably wrong and probably stupid, but her heart was overruling her head. When he was close like this, she couldn't think, and what was more, she didn't even care.

"Dusty Autumn."

His voice woke her with a jolt.

"What?"

Then she realized why he'd said the name. They'd turned to a page with a picture of the two of them, Cam and Dusty, arm in arm and looking like love's eternal couple. He was staring at it, a smile on his face.

Dread filled Ann. "I...I guess you two were pretty serious at one time, weren't you?" Was that strangled sound really her own voice?

Cam was nodding. "She came into my life like a thunderbolt. I took one look at her and I said, 'This is it. This is the one I want.' This was back when I was young, you understand, when I still believed in love at first sight, when I still believed in love, period. Anyway, I fell head over heels and I had a friend get her for me."

"Get her for you? What are you talking about?"

He met her doubtful gaze and touched her cheek lightly with his fingertips.

"Ten years ago was a crazy time for me, Ann. I was feeling my oats. You see, I had made myself into a very important person in a very short time, and I must admit, I had the swelled head to go with it."

"I never knew you were that important." Why had she said that? She sounded defensive again. Her shoulders sagged and she wished she could take back the words.

He smiled, looking at her lips. "You weren't paying attention."

That was true. But in those days, she was trying very consciously not to think about him. She'd heard something about the cover article, but she'd never seen it herself at the time.

He turned back and stared down at the picture.

"Well, I'll tell you, back then, I snapped my fingers and I got what I wanted. I had people running around wherever I went, their only goal in life to make mine as comfortable as possible. I saw Dusty in that little country bar and decided she was the one for me, and to hell with what anyone else thought. I was selfishness personified. I thought I could have whatever I wanted, that the rest of the world was going to have to bend to my wishes. I said, 'Okay, get her for me,' to Junior MacDonald, one of the men who worked for me. Junior went over and told her who I was. She came eagerly enough."

Who wouldn't? Ann could just see him being arrogant. It fit in with her old picture of him. It fit in with the image of the man who had turned his back on Johnny, much better than this present Cam Sterling did.

"I guess I did her some good in the long run. She got famous and got a recording contract and she's hot stuff nowadays. You could say I got her started."

But how did it end? That was what Ann wanted to know about. Was it really over? At times, there was something in his voice as he spoke of Dusty that gave Ann goose bumps, as though there were still an emotional tie there. She had to hear that the ties were all severed beyond repair. Suddenly that was very important to her.

"What finally happened?" she asked hesitantly.

He leaned back and laughed. "I was just wondering if I should tell you about that. It's kind of embarrassing. It illustrates so clearly what a fool I can be sometimes."

Ann's heart skipped a beat. "Oh? What do you mean?" Now she had to know.

"You see, I've gone out with a lot of women in my time. When I was in my twenties, I did some of the sort of playing around I wouldn't do today. But the women were as wild as I was, and I never tried to coax an unwilling partner."

He glanced over at her questioningly. For one of the few times in his life, he cared how a woman read him, what she thought. If she disapproved, he knew it would hurt. This was his life he was laying out for her. If she made a sign that he disgusted her in any way...

He didn't see any evidence of that at all. Her eyes were soft and warm and full of wonder at what he was saying. He wanted to take her in his arms and thank her. He itched to touch her, kiss her....

But no. Just friends. He had to hold on to that, no matter what. He hardened himself and went on.

"Anyway, when I found Dusty and decided I was going to marry her, I made a big mistake. I decided she was so wonderful, so unique, I wouldn't sleep with her until we were married." He glanced at Ann, self-mocking laughter in his eyes. "It was a compliment to her. At least that was the way I looked at it at the time.

I thought I was honoring her by holding back." He chuckled, shaking his head.

"Think again, genius," he quietly chided himself. "I realized my mistake the day I found Dusty in bed with Junior. That certainly blew that dream out of the water."

"Oh, Cam..." Despite everything, her heart broke at the hurt he must have felt and she felt tears stinging.

"That finally opened my eyes. It was as though I suddenly saw the world so much more clearly. I was rich, successful, famous, powerful, and...and everyone around me was only there to bask in the glory and take a little piece of it home for themselves."

He searched her eyes. Could she possibly understand?

"I was paying people like Junior to be my friend. Actually, there was no such thing as a friend. There was no such thing as a lover. It was all commodity, bought and paid for. Or stolen, on the sly."

His voice had taken on a bitter edge and she wanted to reach for him, to comfort him with her love, her body, anything that might work.

But it wasn't like that between them, and she couldn't make the first move. Gutsy as she was in her daily life, she was scared to death of this. Sitting very still, she waited, willing him to touch her.

He closed the scrapbook and laid it aside. When his eyes met hers, she began to tremble, ever so slightly, her body reacting to the adrenaline his nearness released in her. He stared at her for a moment, then dragged his gaze away from her eyes and reached out to gather her hair in his hand.

"Ann."

He was so close. She could hear his ragged breathing and she turned toward him expectantly, yearningly.

"Cam," she whispered, and she took his hand and raised it to her lips, kissing the palm, then turning her face so that her cheek was pressed there. Closing her eyes, she waited, letting the moment stretch into forever.

But it didn't do that.

She felt his hand move, beginning to draw away, and when she opened her eyes and looked into his, she saw a deep, abiding regret, and then he was pulling away from her, leaning away so that their shoulders wouldn't touch, rejecting her.

She sat very still, stung. A buzzing filled her ears and she could hardly hear his next words.

"I think you can understand why this whole thing about Johnny has really gotten to me."

In a fog, she barely made out what he was saying. What? Johnny? What was he talking about?

"For so many years I couldn't trust anyone or anything. I really didn't have any friends I could count on. In fact, I think I forgot what a real friend was."

He was coming in more clearly now, but she still didn't know why he was saying these things. She stared at him and awaited revelation.

"You reminded me of what a friend was all about when you made me remember Johnny. I...I can't tell you how much I regret not having kept in touch with him. I'll never forgive myself for that."

She felt as though she were curling up into a ball.
Why was he bringing Johnny up now? Didn't he realize that put distance between them? Or was this his
purpose?

If she had to remember Johnny, then she had to remember that Cam was the one who betrayed him. And
she had to remember that she herself betrayed him,
with her obsession with Cam. With all that on her
conscience, how could she set herself free?

The answer was, she couldn't. She shuddered and
pulled her arms tightly around herself.

"Ann, you accused me of forgetting my promises to
Johnny. I think you meant that I'd forgotten him, and
you were right. In that way, I let him down."

He took her by the shoulders, gazing into her eyes
with earnest intensity, as though he had to make sure
she was listening.

"Johnny was the best friend I ever had. He's gone.
There's nothing I can do about that. But Ann..." His
voice faltered and he searched her eyes. "Ann, I can
be your friend, if you'll let me."

She stared at him. He wanted to be her friend.
Didn't he understand that wasn't what she wanted at
all?

Embarrassment flooded her. Surely he had noticed
how she had been expecting something else. And he
had tactfully ignored it. She felt heat filling her cheeks
and she looked away.

"Of course we can be friends," she said quickly. "I
would really like that. Of course."

He looked relieved and he was going to say something else, but she didn't think she wanted to hear it.

"I . . . I'm really tired, though, Cam. I think I'll go to bed now."

She smiled at him and rose, starting back into the kitchen. She didn't want to talk to Cam any longer. She didn't know what she could possibly say.

He wanted to be her friend. Here she'd been fighting this growing attraction, sure that it was just about as strong on his side as it was on hers. And when she finally began to give in to it, she'd found out that all he wanted was to be her friend.

Worse still, she knew it wasn't about liking her. It was about making things up to Johnny.

She couldn't think, couldn't even feel, didn't have the slightest idea what she was doing. She was so tired. So tired. All she wanted to do was get into bed and sleep for hours, days.

But she didn't go to bed. She walked on through the kitchen and out into the yard, and out across the grass, toward the trees, walking on and on, her mind racing, going over one thing after another, but revealing nothing at all that was in any way coherent.

She had no idea how long she walked. She was almost back to the house when she heard Bobby's truck return. She could hear the country music playing loudly as the vehicle approached, and then it disappeared when the engine went off, and there was Bobby coming toward her.

"Well, I went and got myself lost," Bobby told her cheerfully.

Ursula was walking behind him, her eyes rather wild. "We rode in that horrible contraption for hours," she said, clutching at Ann's arm and leaning against her shoulder. "I didn't know what was going to happen to me."

"Oh, come on now, it wasn't that bad," Bobby said with a happy grin. "We did find some windy roads, I will say that. But I stopped and got you a nice drink, now didn't I?"

Ursula shuddered, holding Ann in a death grip, as though she were a life preserver. "He took me to this horrible grimy little bar."

"Oh, hey, now don't you go calling Duke's Country Swing names. It's a nice country and western club, and I work there."

"He sang me hillbilly songs right in front of everybody."

"And they clapped. They don't clap for things they don't like in there." Bobby shook his head, his dark eyes sparkling with humor. "But I've gotta say, Ursula sure did disappoint me. She keeps talking about what a good horsewoman she is and here she wouldn't even ride the mechanical bull."

Ursula raised her head from Ann's shoulder. "That horrible thing that kept bobbing up and down?" Straightening to her full height, she glared at Bobby. "It'll be a cold day in hell, mister, before I let anyone humiliate me on one of those things."

Tossing her head, she flounced off toward the house.

Ann looked at Bobby and she didn't know whether to laugh at Ursula or cry from weariness.

"She is all right, isn't she?" she asked a bit anxiously.

"There's nothing ailing her that couldn't be cured," he drawled. "I just may make it my goal for the summer to get her on that bull."

Ann's laugh was cut short when she heard Cam's voice coming from behind her.

"I have to thank you, Bobby. You did me a big favor."

"Hey, no big deal."

"You're going to stay, aren't you? We've got rooms just sitting empty. And I'd enjoy having you around."

"Well, I'll tell you, I think you've talked me into it. That little room I've been staying in down in town just doesn't have the appeal this place has." His grin was boyishly enthusiastic. "Staying here would be great."

While they were still talking, making plans and deciding what room Bobby would take, she slipped away, hurrying to the house. When she looked back she could see Cam looking after her. But she didn't wave.

Seven

If this was what being friends was going to be like, Ann thought they might as well go back to being wary acquaintances. It had been a whole lot more comfortable.

True, Cam was around more these days. But he treated her with such an artificial heartiness it made her squirm. Instead of the easy, slightly barbed banter she had become used to, now she got sports metaphors and jocular pats on the back. She was just waiting for him to grab a football and yell at her to go out for a long one.

There were friends, and then there were friends. Someone was going to have to clue Cam in to the difference.

In the meantime, the work on the parties went on.

"Has there been a decision on the theme for the next party?" she asked a few days after the luau.

Cam scowled but didn't protest going on with the themes.

"With Bobby here," he said instead, "well, what do you think? A country hoedown, of course."

She'd nodded and smiled. "Yippi-ti-yi-aa," she said softly.

He laughed and added, "Get along, little doggie," and for just a moment, he looked normal again.

But then his eyes changed and his expression stiffened and he said, "Say, how about that Giants game last night?" and he was a "friend" once more.

As a matter of fact, the friend situation was getting out of hand all the way around. Ursula was so friendly, Ann was about to have her tied up and gagged for a while, just to get some peace and quiet.

And good old Bobby was a constant presence. His job took him away in the evenings, but he got up early anyway and was around all day. He was often helpful and always cheerful, but it was a strain sometimes, and his fights with Ursula reached epic proportions.

Ursula was at the Sterling estate to win Cam, and she made no bones about it.

"You see, I know he doesn't love me," she told Ann one afternoon as they both strolled through the garden, taking in the scent of roses in bloom. "But I'm ready to give him everything he wants. He wants children to carry on the name, and a wife who stays out of his way. I can do that. I can do both. I have my own life. I don't need his to make me happy."

She looked as sincere as a missionary setting off for China. Ann gazed at her in wonder.

"But why do *you* need *him*?" she asked.

Ursula stopped to trim off a dead blossom and pursed her lips. "I'm ready to marry. He's just the sort of man I need. And we've been betrothed—" she snapped off the branch with a savage yank "—for years and years. So it's only logical that we go ahead with it."

"What if . . . what if he doesn't agree?"

Ursula looked at her, her eyes shining like those of any saint with a conscience so totally clear, she could not conceive of guilt. "But that would be illogical. He must agree. It's what I'm here for."

When she wasn't following Cam around, she was trying to ditch Bobby. That became more and more difficult, because Cam tended to wrangle Bobby into taking Ursula off his hands whenever possible.

Ursula liked a morning ride and tried to get Cam to accompany her. Instead, she found Bobby saddled and ready to go when she went to the stables.

She came back to the house, fuming and foaming and using bad words.

"Come on, Ursula," Cam said soothingly. "Don't be a spoilsport. You'll enjoy going with him. Bobby can ride like a son of a gun."

Ursula spit fire. "No, Bobby rides like a gorilla on a camel. I won't be seen with him."

"Who's going to see you at six o'clock in the morning?"

"Someone might. I won't take the chance."

But she was finally forced to take that very chance, or give up the idea of riding at all. And when they got back, her cheeks were very pink and she wasn't sputtering any longer.

Ann found herself visiting her little house less often. There was just so much to do at the Sterling estate, and so many people to do it with. When she did get home, her things were beginning to seem less familiar. In some ways, she could see her setting from a distance she'd never achieved before.

For one thing, she noticed how many pictures of Johnny she still had around. She picked up the one in the bedroom, the sad one, and it tore at her heart. Johnny hadn't always been sad. It had been just toward the end, the last six months or so. Why did she keep this picture around when there were so many others?

She rummaged through the box where she kept things like that and found an earlier picture, one where Johnny was laughing and sunshine was filling his face. After slipping the sad picture out of its frame, she replaced it with the laughing one and set it beside her bed.

That was better. Much better. That was the way she should remember him. And she found herself smiling back at the picture, her heart suddenly much lighter than it had been.

Cam sat at dinner and looked down the long dining room table at Ursula and Ann at the other end. His fork had barely touched the poached salmon. He just wasn't hungry.

Ann and Ursula were chatting away, just out of earshot. Bobby was going on and on about the relative merits of motorcycles, but Cam wasn't listening to a word of it. He couldn't get his mind focused on anything but Ann.

This "friends" business wasn't working out as he thought it would. He could easily be friends with Ursula, and he didn't even like her very much. But with Ann, it just wasn't working.

Every time he opened his mouth around her, he sounded like some sleazy politician trying to convince the public of his morals.

Why couldn't he be natural with her any longer? Whenever he had to speak to her, he felt like a big, clumsy buffoon who couldn't remember which fork to use.

Bobby said something he didn't notice and the next thing he knew, the four of them were repairing to the billiard room for a game of pool. He walked behind Ann, watching the way her hair swayed against her back. Was it his imagination, or was she wearing it loose more often now? He loved it that way. It made him want to bury his face . . .

No, damn it! Just friends. He had to remember that.

Bobby racked up the balls and broke, but all Cam saw was the ebony black of Ann's hair against her peach-colored blouse. She turned and her blouse fell open enough to expose her neck. He wanted to press his face there, wanted it with a physical ache that hurt. His fingers tightened on the cue stick until his knuckles were white.

This wasn't what friends were for.

He took his turn, missing his shot and hardly noticing.

Ann did a better job, working her way around the table, talking and laughing with the others, glancing at him now and then as though she were curious as to why he was so quiet and so strained.

Suddenly she accidently bumped into him, her hair swinging against him, some of it whispering against his face. He closed his eyes. He wanted her more than he had ever wanted anything—and not as a friend.

He'd wanted her from the first time he'd really seen her, when he'd kissed her at the senior picnic, all those years ago. What on earth was taking him so long?

She'd been living under his roof for weeks. She was sleeping only a thin door away.

And still the background between them was holding him back. He couldn't get his mind back on business until he got this damn obsession to stop cluttering up his brain.

"I won." She was smiling at him, her eyes glowing in the lamplight, and he felt as though his insides were melting.

Very carefully, he put down the cue stick and left the room. There was only so much a man could take.

The hoedown was blazing along, going hell-for-leather, and Cam was the life of the party, dancing and joking and having a wonderful time.

Or was he?

If the truth was known, his mind was hardly on a thing he was doing or saying. He moved from one lady to the next, and with every one he had to admit to himself again that there wasn't a woman present he could ever, ever want the way he wanted Ann.

At one point, he turned and saw her with Bobby. Bobby was laughing, leaning toward her, obviously teasing her, and a searing slash of jealousy ripped through Cam's chest. For just a second, he wanted to tear Bobby's head off, even though he knew, when given a few more seconds to reflect, that there was no real attraction between the two of them.

He couldn't go on this way. He was going to have to do something about it.

True, he owed it to Johnny to protect his girl. But did that really mean he couldn't touch her? What if she wanted to be touched? After all, Johnny had been dead for almost ten years. Surely he didn't expect Ann to mourn him indefinitely.

That brought up an interesting point. Someday, Ann was going to choose a new man to have in her life. It was inevitable. Would Johnny really have preferred a complete stranger to the man he had considered his best friend in high school?

Of course not. A new excitement tingled in Cam's veins. This would take some thinking over, but all in all, he knew it was time for a new focus.

He would never hurt Ann. God knows, that was the last thing he would ever want to do. But this hands-off policy was driving him crazy. It had to go.

The hoedown was another success. Ann could hardly believe Mrs. Sterling could round up a hundred eligible females who hadn't been to the previous party, but it seemed there was an inexhaustible supply. They streamed in and they streamed out. It seemed as though Cam danced with every one of them. Ann worked hard and pretended not to notice. And when it was over, she cleaned up and went to bed before Cam could catch her for another postmortem.

But she might as well have saved herself the effort. The next morning, Cam showed up at her door bright and early, a tray with coffee and croissants in his hand.

He was wearing jeans and a tight red polo shirt that let his muscles display themselves nicely. She had to look twice to make sure she wasn't still dreaming. But no. There he was.

She watched him close the door and come into the room. Her eyes were wide, her hair wild, her covers pulled up as tightly as possible under her chin.

He seemed unbearably cheerful for so early an hour. What did that mean? Had he struck pay dirt last night? Had he at last found a woman he was willing to make a commitment to? Was there a wedding in the offing?

She found that all hard to believe, and yet why was he grinning at her like this? Why the celebratory croissants?

"Sit up and eat," he ordered, putting the tray down on her nightstand. "You're going to need your strength." He strode over and yanked open her drapes, flooding the room with sunshine.

She squinted painfully and sank deeper into her covers.

"It's too early," she grumbled, her voice projecting from under the depths of bed linen.

"It's never too early," he announced, sitting down on the edge of her bed and slapping a folder full of papers on her pillow. He peered into the twisted tangle of sheets and comforters, trying to find her.

"What are you doing down there? Playing possum?"

"Go away. I want to sleep."

He plunged his hands down into the covers, not so much searching for body parts as trying to find a handhold to pull her back up. But his fingers made contact with her soft breast and he heard her gasp. His hand lingered just a second longer and his stomach seemed to fall away. God, but she was soft and sweet and—he bit his lip and forced his hand to move, catching hold of her shoulder and tugging gently.

"Listen to me, Ann Dupree," he drawled. "I've been very good for a very long time. You had better watch out, because when I'm bad, I can get very bad."

She moved her head and looked up at him with her one uncovered eye. "What do you do when you get very bad?" she asked softly.

His smile was definitely wicked. "I get very, very good," he said silkily. "Do you want an example?"

"No!" She came up out of the covers, so that at least her head was cleared, eyeing him doubtfully.

Was she still asleep, or had that sounded very much like the old Cam she had known and been crazy about for so long? Was the "friend" really gone? Or was this just an illusion brought on by her fevered longings?

"What are you doing here, anyway?"

He sat back and grinned at her. "We've got work to do. I need help going through the prospects from last night."

She frowned, blinking the sleep away. "Then you still haven't found your perfect match?"

He patted the folder. "She just may be right in here."

Ann turned her head and looked at the folder suspiciously. "What do you mean?"

"I decided I wasn't getting anywhere with my slap-dash methods. I needed a more professional approach. So I had Bobby going around with an instant camera, taking pictures of every female present."

"You're kidding."

"Not at all. I've got them all right here. We can go through them and put them into piles."

Ann groaned. "Don't you think you could go do that all by yourself in your own little room?"

"No." His smile was crooked. "Actually, I need help. I need a woman's touch. You probably know a lot more about women than I do. So. Let's begin." He looked at her expectantly.

She knew she looked awful—no makeup, straggly hair. But what the heck? They were only friends, right?

Slowly, she emerged from the covers until she was sitting up against the fluffy pillows, glad that she'd worn her best lacy nightgown at least.

She glanced at the food and drink on the tray and shuddered. Somehow, hunger was not an issue at the moment.

"All right, Cam," she said a bit hoarsely. "Let's get this over with."

"Here we go." He shook out the pictures and began picking them up at random.

"Meg Marlowe. The all-American sports woman. Look at those calf muscles. I think she's even got bulging biceps. She can run, shoot and surf, but her favorite pastime is lacrosse. What do you think?"

Ann looked at the picture and wondered if that throbbing at her temples was a headache coming on.

"I don't know, Cam. This might just be that sporty playmate you've been looking for."

He considered for a moment, staring at the picture. "Naw, I hate lacrosse," he said at last. "She goes in the 'Regrets Only' pile."

Ann smiled and shook her hair back. Maybe it wasn't so straggly, after all. He was looking at her as though he liked what he saw. And best of all, that horrible guarded look was gone.

"Who's next?"

"Sheri Kat." He presented the picture and let out a low whistle. "Look at that face."

Ann winced and hated her, but was determined not to show it. "She's certainly beautiful."

"Oh yeah, she's beautiful." He sighed. "She's also thick as a brick."

"She looks perfectly intelligent to me."

"You've obviously never spoken to the woman. Her entire conversation consists of 'like, I was all, you know' and 'no dah!'"

Ann made a face. "Okay. Regrets for her, as well."

He pulled out another one. "Priscilla Akvid. Look at this. Is this pioneer stock, or what? Can't you just see her leading the wagons across the plains, a rifle over her shoulder and a baby at her breast?"

"Put this in the 'Consider' pile. Just in case you want to open up a new frontier someday."

"Now here's little Sally Saugas. Isn't she cute? She whispered sweet nothings in my ear while we danced."

"What kind of sweet nothings?" Ann was suspicious.

"Oh...promises of sexual splendor such as I've never even imagined. I maybe ought to ask this one out for a few more meetings."

Ann grabbed the picture and tossed it. "'Regrets Only,'" she said. "We are looking for lifemates here. Not bimbos."

Major disappointment. "No bimbos?"

"No. Not even mini-bimbos." She pawed through the pictures looking for a face she might recognize, but the women who had attended the night before had been a blur to her. She stopped and faced Cam with a question.

"What I don't understand is...why do all these women want you?"

He looked downright hurt by her puzzlement. "What do you mean, why do they want me?"

"What makes them come in droves like they do?"

"Listen, do I have to sell myself to you? I'm darn good-looking, in case you hadn't noticed."

She shrugged and made a face. "There are other handsome men."

He considered that for a moment and had to agree. "Well, I've got a lot of money."

She shook her head, frowning. "Most of these women already have money themselves."

He was beginning to look as puzzled as she was. "Maybe it's because I was famous for a while."

"That was ten years ago."

"Well, maybe...maybe it's because I'm kinda cuddly." He smiled as he thought of that, pleased with himself.

She wasn't ready to accept it, though. "Cuddly?" she repeated, skepticism dripping from her tone.

He gave her his superior look. "You haven't tried it out, so you wouldn't know."

She shook her head slowly. "Chubby guys are cuddly," she informed him.

"What? I'm not fat enough for you?"

"Well..."

"I'm not exactly skinny. Here, look at this."

He tugged up his shirt and showed off his washboard belly. He certainly wasn't skinny, but neither was there an ounce of fat. Smooth tanned skin rippled under a coating of golden hair. "What do you think of that?" he asked.

She took a deep breath and looked away. "Cam! No striptease this early in the morning."

"No? I was hoping we could do a duet."

Her gaze flew back and searched his laughing eyes. This was certainly the old Cam back again, sassy and sexy and teasing. What had happened to "just friends"?

"Let's stick to the subject," she said cautiously. She wasn't sure she could trust this turn of events. "Tell me just what else you have to offer these women. What kind of a husband do you plan to make, anyway?"

"I'm going to be a great husband."

"Really?" She raised an eyebrow and waited.

He looked worried. "Okay, okay. What does a great husband do, exactly?"

"He provides for the family."

"I can do that."

"He protects the family from harm."

"No problem."

"He is loving support for his wife."

He started to answer that one as quickly as he had answered the others, but before he got the words out, he stopped and frowned. "What does that mean, exactly? I mean, I can't imagine myself propping up old Meg Marlowe for too long."

"Not physical support. Emotional support."

Still he hesitated. "Okay, give me an example."

"All right. Let's say your wife has a bad day at the office—"

"Office! My wife won't have to work."

"Oh? What are you? Some kind of sexist? Your wife can't have a job if she wants one? She's just supposed to stay home and stare out the window waiting for you to show up?"

"Why not? That's what I'll be paying her for."

"What? If that's the way you think about it, why don't you just advertise for a wife in the employment section of the classified ads?"

His eyes sparkled with a devilish light. "Why? Are you looking for a job?"

She rolled her eyes and shook her head. "Not me. We're talking about the candidates."

"Oh." He seemed to be disappointed.

She pretended to be exasperated. "Okay, we'll do it your way. Say your wife has burned the brownies."

"Much better."

"She's sitting there, sobbing her little heart out when you come home. What do you do?"

"That's easy. Turn pale. Back out the door. Round up a racquetball partner and play at least two hours until she can get herself together." He looked pleased with himself. "Wouldn't that be thoughtful?"

Ann's look was filled with scorn. "Not a bit. How is she supposed to get herself together when she's alone in the house with nothing but burned brownies for company? What's going to help make her happier?"

"I...I could stop by a bakery on the way home from the racquetball game."

"No. She needs your emotional support. She needs your shoulder to cry on. You have to come on into the house, take her little face against your shoulder, pat her back and say, 'There, there, it's all right.'"

He was frowning doubtfully.

"Here," she said, gesturing for him to move closer. "Try it." She pretended to be crying and he took her into his arms.

He tried to ignore the warm flesh beneath the lacy fabric, the rich, lemony smell of her hair.

"There, there," he said, patting her clumsily. "It's all right. I don't like brownies anyway."

Her head swung back so that she could look him in the face. "Not quite," she informed him a bit breathlessly.

He didn't let go of her, but he didn't say anything, and she wet her lips and told him, "The thing that would be best to do, and the thing that seems least likely..."

She stared up at him, wondering if she dared to say it.

"What's that?" he asked.

She took a deep breath and said, very softly, "You could love her."

He stared at her, his fingers pressing on her shoulders. Slowly, he began to shake his head from side to side.

"This is too hard. I can't do this."

She had no idea what he was talking about. "What?" she asked, searching his face for a clue.

"Fall in love with any of those women." He looked pained. "Why can't I just marry someone I like? Someone like . . . you, for instance."

"Me?" she heard herself echoing. Her pulse was beginning to speed up. "Why me?"

"Why not you? I don't think I know anyone I like better."

Great. More liking. What ever happened to loving? Or was that a concept he was still unclear on?

But right now, she didn't care very much. All she could see was the hard line of his jaw, the crystal blue of his eyes, the shiny darkness of his lashes, and all she could feel was his hard, beautiful body coming closer again.

His hand slid into her hair, tilting her head so that her lips were accessible. She felt herself part them, waiting for him, her heart beating so loudly, the room might have been rocking from an earthquake.

He came to her quickly, as though he didn't want to let her ponder it a moment more, fearing she would reconsider and pull away. He didn't want to think and he didn't want her to think. There was too much thinking in their relationship as it was. It was time to feel.

The feeling was hot, the feeling was fire. He wanted to touch all of her, her hair, her skin, her breasts. His hands moved across her back and down, cupping her bottom, and at the same time, his body pressed hers until he was lying with her against the pillows. Her nightgown was light and filmy and he could feel her beneath the cloth. The need for her became a throbbing drive that threatened to consume him.

"Ann," he whispered against her mouth. "Oh God, you're so beautiful."

He kissed her again and she forgot how to breathe. She didn't need air any longer, she only needed him and the touch of his hand on her breast, tender and slightly rough through the lace. She moved as though she were in a dream, and in that dream, anything was possible.

Cam felt her body respond to his touch and he lost his head. He hadn't meant to take things this far this fast, but he was in no mood to remember caution right now. His hand slid down between her legs, and suddenly she was jerking away from him, pulling out of his arms, leaving him behind.

He looked up, groggy, needing to refocus just to come back to earth.

"Whoa," she murmured, staring at him as she pulled her nightgown back the way it was supposed to go. Her eyes were very wide, her lips stinging from his kiss. "Too much, too soon."

"I disagree," he returned, clearing his throat with effort. "Too little, too late."

He reached for her again, but she avoided him and spun off the bed.

"What happened to all that 'just good friends' business?" she asked, backing toward the bathroom, her arms folded protectively across her chest.

He shrugged, watching her, his eyes cloudy with confused emotions. "I'm a failure as a friend," he told her softly. "But I think I could make it as a lover."

She stopped, hand on the knob to the bathroom. "Let me know when you think you can juggle both at the same time," she told him, her hair hanging over her eyes. "*That* I might be interested in."

And then she disappeared behind the closed door and he sat very still, staring at where she had been.

Eight

"You've got to get me out of these parties."

Ann raised an eyebrow as she put the folder of pictures down in front of where Cam sat at the desk in the library. He had left them in the room that morning without going through any more of the prospects. So much for his new, businesslike approach to finding a mate by instant camera work.

"Talk to your mother," she advised.

He groaned, running a hand through his hair. "Haven't you noticed? I have a real hard time saying 'no' to my mother. Can't you do it?"

"Cam!" She sank down into the chair on the other side of the desk and leaned on it. Strange, but it felt perfectly natural to do so. The employer-employee relationship had been abandoned long ago—if it had ever existed in anything but name, anyway. "You know I can't do a thing about this."

She gazed at him speculatively. Was he serious? And what did it all mean?

"Why do you want to stop the parties, anyway?"

He let his gaze drift slowly over her crisp, clean appearance, enjoying the sight of her. She'd pulled her hair back into a tight bun and put on a navy blue blouse and white linen slacks. She looked very efficient. She also looked absolutely delicious.

"I can't bear any more of these parties. There's no point to them. I'm not going to marry any of these women. I thought I might be able to, but when it comes right down to it, I know I can't."

This was all very welcome news; still Ann felt a little uneasy. There seemed to be something missing.

"What about Ursula?" she asked him. "She seems to think she has the inside track."

"With my mother, not with me." He laughed shortly. "Mother can marry her if she likes. I never will."

Ann nodded. "Poor Ursula," she murmured.

He glared at her. "When I was a kid, Ursula was at every birthday party, even though she was five years younger than I was. I had to take Ursula to the movies when I was seventeen and she was only twelve. Ursula has been the bane of my existence all my life. Marrying Ursula would be like marrying my childhood nightmare."

He shook his head, frowning. "But it's not much different with the others. You know, I thought I could treat this marriage thing like a business deal, but now I know I can't."

She nodded, waiting for him to go on. She had to know his motivations. Was this just a retreat to past positions—or something new?

When he didn't add anything, she asked, very softly, "Are you still so afraid of making a commitment? Of making a real connection to another human being?"

He recoiled a bit, then relaxed. "I have been in the past, I know." Taking her hand, he stared at her fingers. "But I don't think that's a problem anymore."

He looked up and met her eyes, and suddenly she was the one who was wary. She wasn't sure exactly what he meant. She knew there was a sexual attraction between the two of them that charged each encounter they had with a dangerous electricity. But what did it all mean? She had no idea.

"Are you sure you know what you're looking for?" she asked him. "Maybe if you got a better focus on your needs..."

He used her arm to pull her toward him until their faces were very close across the corner of the desk. "I understand my needs quite well," he said.

She couldn't help but smile, feeling his breath on her face. "Maybe it would help if you learned to differentiate between 'needs' and 'wants,'" she told him. "If you just had a better idea of what you want in a wife..."

His kiss stopped her words and she responded. It was gentle but provocative, and it lasted only a moment. But it served to completely wipe all thought from her head, and she emerged a bit breathless, and not sure what they were talking about.

"Will you back me up?" he asked her earnestly. "I'll talk to my mother tonight. I'll call a meeting in the solarium. Okay?"

It took a moment for Ann to get back into the swing. "Uh . . . you're going to talk to her about stopping the parties?"

"Yes."

"You won't even let her have the one this Friday? She's been planning for it with so much excitement."

"Ann." He looked at her helplessly. "You're looking at a drowning man here."

She laughed, touching his cheek. It was lovely feeling this free with him, this important to him. "Hardly that. But I'll help you, if I can."

He leaned forward to kiss her again, but she backed away. "This could get to be a habit," she warned him.

He nodded happily. "I was hoping just that." He took her chin in his hand and contemplated her lips. "I'm trying to prove to you that I can meet your standards."

She blinked but didn't pull away. "What standards?"

"Being both friend and lover at the same time." He dropped a quick kiss, then grinned at her. "That was from the friend. Now here's the lover."

She was laughing, so her defenses were practically nonexistent, and as the kiss deepened, and his arms came around her, she melted against him, amazed at the feelings he aroused in her so easily.

Friend and lover. Yes, she could sense them both. And she loved them both. So where did that leave her?

When the kiss was over, she stayed snuggled against his chest. He stroked her hair, and she never wanted to leave the protection of his arms again.

"Your mother could walk in at any moment," she reminded him, sighing.

"That's okay." He caught her hand in his own and began to kiss her fingers. "My mother likes you."

She giggled. "Your mother likes Ursula."

"Well, yes, but she likes you second best. I'm pretty sure you're ahead of Dusty, anyway."

"Dusty?" Ann's face changed and her head rose from where it had been resting against his chest. "Did you . . . did your mother meet her?"

"Sure. I brought her home . . . once. And my mother liked her, to my surprise."

Ann pulled all the way out of his arms, pretending to be looking for something on the desk, but really just needing this bit of distance at the moment. "Did she?"

"Yeah, with certain reservations. I was almost disappointed in how much she liked her. I guess I had this idea in my head that marrying Dusty would provide some kind of little rebellion for me, kind of like the rebellion when I forced Mom to let me go to public high school. You know?"

"I think I understand."

"Dusty didn't like it here much. I guess it reminded her too much of the little Texas town she grew up in. She was anxious to get back to New York right away, so we didn't stay long. She was kind of addicted to the bright lights, Broadway, the opera, parties, the shops." He sighed. "It used to make me laugh, the way she would crow when she found her name in the society pages. I was used to it by then. It didn't mean a thing to me. But it meant everything to her. She loved to see her name in print."

He shook his head, remembering, a faint smile on his lips.

Ann watched him, feeling just a bit afraid. "Cam," she probed tentatively, "are you still in love with Dusty?"

"Dusty?" He stared at her blankly, then laughed. "Oh no, no," he said shaking his head emphatically. "No, that was over the minute I found her with Junior. Believe me. All feeling I had for Dusty died an untimely death."

That was certainly a relief. She believed him implicitly. In fact, she always took whatever he said as the truth. The only times she was uneasy were when she was pretty sure he was fooling himself, or unable to face something.

"Have you heard from her since then?" she asked him.

"Not really. I haven't seen anyone from those days until I hooked up with Bobby again."

He had opened up to her with so much of himself, things she had a feeling he had never revealed to anyone else. And yet, she felt hesitant about asking questions. He might think she was going too far. And at the same time, there were things that had to be cleared up between them.

Steeling herself, she said, "You said the other night that...that what happened with Dusty made you cynical about friendship."

He looked at her, his eyes dark as midnight lakes. "That's right. It was just one of many instances that soured me. But it was a doozy. The thing that broke the camel's back, I guess."

"Is that why...? Cam, I have to ask you this, because it's been on my mind for ten years and I have to know the answer."

He waited, nodding slowly and saying, "Go on."

She was trembling. This wasn't easy. It cut very close to the bone.

"Is that why you turned Johnny down when he wrote you about the loan? Because you thought he was just another person trying to grab a piece of you?"

Cam's face was completely blank.

"Ann," he said slowly, beginning to frown. "I don't know what you're talking about."

She took a trembling breath. "Don't you remember? It was just ten years ago last March. Johnny's father had died and his mother moved to Florida. He was in charge of the store. And it was going under. We were desperate. Finally, I convinced him to write to you."

She shrugged, holding her palms up toward him. "I didn't know what else to do. No one in town would give him a loan. And we knew you were doing so well in New York."

Cam was shaking his head. "Ann, I swear to God, I never got that letter. I would have remembered that. Lord, I would have sent money so fast!" He winced, thinking of how much he would have wanted to help Johnny. "Oh, Ann, are you sure?"

"Yes. I saw him mail it."

Cam buried his face in his hands, thinking hard. Suddenly, he lifted his gaze to hers again. "Of course.

What am I thinking of? That whole year, when I was on the cover of that magazine and got so famous and all, I hired a public relations firm to handle my mail. I was getting tons of letters every day, most of them asking for something. I couldn't possibly handle it myself. So they screened requests for me."

He reached out and took her hand again, a growing look of horror in his eyes. "Did you ever get a reply?"

She nodded. "A form letter that said you were too busy to write."

He groaned again, his shoulders sagging. "Well, there it is. That's what happened. The secretary at the public relations firm filed Johnny's letter away and I never saw it."

"You...you never saw it?" The words were there but the truth was difficult to digest. After all these years of being so sure Cam had deliberately let Johnny down, to readjust her thinking would take a while.

He never saw it. That meant he hadn't rejected Johnny's plea. He wasn't the cold, unfeeling monster she'd manufactured in her mind all this time. He really was the warm, exciting boy she'd fallen for in high school. He was older, more wary, less spontaneous. But he was the same boy. The boy she'd always loved.

But Johnny... What did this mean to him? He'd died thinking his friend had deserted him. If only he had known, if only there were some way to tell him...

Tears filled her eyes and she looked away from Cam.

"Ann."

He couldn't bear to see her cry. Rising, he pulled her up into his arms and held her tightly, then looked down and kissed the tears from her face. "Ann, sweet Ann, don't cry," he murmured, heart aching.

Oh God, he thought, anguish coursing through him. She still loves him. How could he ever compete with a ghost?

Especially the ghost of the best friend he had ever had.

Encounters with Mrs. Sterling tended to take unpredictable twists and turns, and their meeting that evening in the solarium was no exception.

Ann noticed Maxwell near the doorway and she nodded to him, then slipped into the room where Mrs. Sterling and Cam were already seated on rattan chairs, with potted ferns and orchids by their sides.

"Come in, my dear," Mrs. Sterling said, gesturing for her to come in and sit down. "I was just reminiscing with Cameron about his father. You know, he was such a wonderful man. I only wish he were here to see our son finally marry." For a moment, a wistful look was on her face, then she brightened. "By the way, I am so looking forward to the party Friday. An English tea on the lawn. Won't that be nice? And we're only having twenty of the top candidates who have been with us before. A sort of selection of the best, don't you know. I'm sure you'll find your dream girl from among them."

Cam almost paled. "Oh my God."

"I'm off to order lace napkins," she continued, not having heard Cam's remark.

She left them sitting there, staring at each other, each totally aware that the mission had not been accomplished.

"I don't know if I can take this, Ann."

"Just one more party," Ann said softly. "You can do it."

He shook his head. "I guess there will be one more party," he told her. "But whether or not I will attend it is still up in the air."

She blew him a kiss and left the room. He stayed where he was, staring into a giant fern. What a summer. It certainly was different from the good old days, cruising the Med with interchangeable bathing beauties or living it up in Monte Carlo. Great vacations, those. Like cotton candy—no real substance, no nutritional value, but tasty and fun, and you didn't have to think about anything at all.

What had he done to deserve this summer that was so full of doing things to please his mother, finding out he was riddled with guilt, and falling in love with a woman who made him look at his life in ways that hurt?

He knew what he'd done to deserve it all. A lifetime of making fast bucks and damning the consequences, too many years of living for gain and fame and forgetting to call a friend. He knew he had to pay for that.

But what hurt worse was knowing Johnny had been forced to pay, too.

"Ann, I need your advice." Ursula appeared in the kitchen a few days later to watch Ann icing a tray of petits fours. "How am I going to get Cam to marry me?"

Ann's knife slipped and smashed two of the little cakes flat. It was a moment before she could stabilize and speak normally.

"Ursula, I can't give you advice on that."

"Why not? You seem to know Cam better than all the rest of us put together. He trusts you. Perhaps you can approach him for me."

"Ursula." Ann was shaking her head and laughing softly.

The lovely creature pouted. "He was supposed to treat this like a business deal, darn it. That is certainly how I've tried to handle it. A merger. That is exactly what I need."

Ann stopped what she was doing and stared at the woman. "What are you talking about?"

Ursula sighed. "Well, Ann, I might as well tell you. I need Cam's money. I own a little restaurant in Sausalito."

"A restaurant! So that's why you're always so interested in how I'm running the kitchen."

"Of course. It's been wildly successful. We have to beat off customers with a stick. But it's at that awkward stage—too small to make enough money to support the quality. I need to move to larger facilities. And for that, I need capital."

"But, Ursula, your family—"

"Hate me being in the restaurant business. They turn up their collective noses whenever I mention it."

"What would they like you to do?"

"Stay home and give parties. Help run the house. Organize the staff. My mother is such a flop at that, she can't even find a butler who will work for her, and the maids terrorize her by pretending to go into comas when she asks them to wash windows." Her sigh was heartbreaking. "They won't help. They want to see me fail and come home to take care of them all." She squared her shoulders. "And that, I refuse to do." She frowned. "I was really counting on marrying Cam and getting his cash. Darn it."

A thought occurred to her. "Wait a minute. Here's an avenue I hadn't considered before. I wonder... Do you suppose I could make a deal with Cam's mother?" Her eyes were bright as a bird's. "He's a cream puff where that lady is concerned. Now if I can just think of the right button to push..."

She wandered off, leaving Ann to stare after her, a flutter of panic in her chest. Ursula was right. He was a pushover for his mother. He would do almost anything for her.

"But not this, Cam," she whispered. "Not this."

Ann and Cam hardly had a moment alone together for the rest of the week. That was just as well. Ann's emotions were in such confusion where Cam was concerned, she didn't seem to have the strength to sort things out.

The only thing she knew for certain was that she was in love. The sound of his voice sent her pulse into a tailspin. The sight of him caught her heart in her throat. And when he came close enough to touch her, the buzzing in her ears was deafening.

She was totally and completely and crazily in love with Cam. But then, she always had been, hadn't she?

She knew she was going to have to leave soon. She could hardly keep working at finding a woman for the man she loved, could she? Besides, she knew Cam wasn't going to tolerate another party after the tea on Friday. And that meant she was out of a job.

She loved Cam. She wanted to be near him, to hear him, to sense his presence in her day. So... where did they go from here?

She had no idea. Cam needed a wife. But he didn't want a love-match. He wanted a business arrangement.

Besides, would she marry him, even if he wanted her to? The thought of marrying, of replacing Johnny, made her feel slightly sick to her stomach. There was still too much guilt curling the edges of her happiness.

For she *was* happy. Just being in love with Cam made her happy. Just being near him, talking to him, hearing him in the next room, filled her day. And it seemed to make him happy, too.

Still, she knew instinctively that it wouldn't be long before they would both need something more.

Rain threatened all day Friday, but they prepared for tea on the lawn anyway, stringing paper lanterns and setting out lovely place settings at little tables placed all up and down the yard.

"It's going to rain," Ann warned, looking at the sky.

"It wouldn't dare," Mrs. Sterling retorted, refusing to glance up at all.

The first fat drops of water started to fall as the long, white limousines began to arrive. Ann stood and watched stoically as the lanterns began to sag and the paper decorations at the place settings began to wilt.

"We'll move it all indoors," Mrs. Sterling bellowed, organizing the servants as though she were a general directing a raid on enemy territory.

"She loves adversity," Cam commented dryly, standing beside Ann and watching the select group of candidates arriving. "We'll hear stories about her ingenuity in the face of thundershowers for years to come."

"*You'll* hear them." Ann looked up into his face. "You and your wife."

He looked down into her eyes and for a moment he thought he would never be able to look away again. His left hand reached out and took her hand, and they stood there together just inside the entrance as the women began to come in.

Ann looked lovely, her black hair full and flowing about shoulders left bare by the gauzy white dress she wore. The dress was simple, her jewelry nonexistent, and yet she stood out among this crowd of wealthy dressed-up dolls like an angel among a crowd of beggars.

Ann smiled as she saw the wonder in his eyes. It was odd to be standing there, hand in hand with Cam as the women who were vying to take that hand themselves came through the doorway and saw them there. He was hers, and yet he was not hers at all. But the startled looks didn't seem to bother him. And they certainly didn't bother her.

Tonight's crop was special. These were the one's Mrs. Sterling had liked the best, and also the ones deemed the most serious contenders. The fluff who had just come along for the fun of it had supposedly been eliminated. Tonight they were down to the real competitors.

She recognized some of the ladies from the pictures Cam had showed her.

Sheri Kat, she recalled, was pretty and dumb. She was even prettier tonight in a low-cut gown and diamonds, and she stopped to greet Cam, not noticing Ann at all.

"Like, Sally says tonight's the big night," she said, sounding every inch the bubblehead Cam claimed she was. "And I was all, 'well, for sure, I'll be there,' you know?"

Cam raised an eyebrow. "I don't know how these rumors get started," he commented to Ann as Sheri went on in. "Do you suppose my mother has been telling these women something I don't know."

"Count on it," Ann replied.

Rumor or not, the women all seemed to sense this was a climactic night. As Cam put it, "These ladies look as though they have all come loaded for bear."

They were showing more cleavage, more leg and more sparkling carats than ever before, and altogether they made a dazzling display.

A raven-haired beauty came in, looked at the handholding with a sniff of disdain, and leaned close to Cam.

"I hear tonight is the night of the big decision. I'd like to get you alone and go over the options before you make your final choice. There are things about me you ought to know." She batted her eyes meaningfully and gave him an elaborate wink. Then she nodded at him, just a word to the wise, and he nodded back, feeling like a fool.

"What has my mother gotten me into here?" he muttered.

Meg Marlowe, she of the awesome calves, was next through the door. She grabbed Cam's free hand and frowned at him fiercely. "I hear we're going to be having contests for you later on tonight," she said. "Listen, make sure arm wrestling is in there, because I can win that one."

"Is she planning to pin me to the floor, do you suppose?" Cam worried. He frowned. "You don't think she's got room for a rope in that purse, do you? I'm getting really nervous about this."

Ann smiled, loving him, hating the circus he was going to have to go through. But her smile faded fast as Sally Saugas vamped up to Cam.

"Remember my promise, Cammy?" she purred, leaning toward him the way a cat rubbed against handy legs. "You can take me up on that raincheck tonight, if you've got the nerve." She looked back over her shoulder as she left, sashaying all the way.

"Whew." He pretended to wipe his brow. "I'm not sure I can take much more of this."

He looked at the room full of women. There was something different about them tonight. They had the feel of a fight crowd. They expected action this time.

"You know what?" he muttered to Ann. "The firepower in there is awesome. They've certainly brought out their big . . . guns for the evening, haven't they?"

Ann nodded, feeling worse and worse. She could hardly believe she'd been involved in this campaign. Suddenly, it all seemed so sordid. "Cam?" she said, looking up at him.

But he didn't hear her. He was staring at the women gathering in the room. Why were they coming? Other than Ursula, none of them really knew him. None of them really cared about him, or who he really was. Just more leeches—that was all they were. They just wanted to grab a bit of fame and fortune, just like everybody else. He wasn't a big media star anymore, but after all, he had been once, and he supposed, in some eyes, that was better than nothing. For a fleeting moment, he actively despised them all.

All except Ann. She stood beside him like a princess, quietly proud, sweetly beautiful. How lucky he was that he had found her again.

Ann was staring at the women, too. There were only twenty women invited tonight. Twenty possibilities. She had watched them arriving, each one beautiful, successful, wealthy—and they all wanted Cam. What on earth did she have to offer him that came anywhere near what these women had?

What did he really want from her? What did she want from him?

His mother called him into the room and he left Ann standing where she was. Thunder shook the house. Rain was pouring down now. Ann looked outside and found herself walking out into it. She had to get away. She couldn't bear the marriage mart any longer.

"Where are you going?" Ursula called after her.

"Out for a loaf of bread," she called back. "Don't wait up."

She was soaked to the skin by the time she got to the old brick caretaker's cottage. She hadn't really meant to come there. She'd thought she would wander in the rain for hours and hours and think things through. But a few moments in the driving rain had changed her mind, and she'd headed for the closest shelter she could find that was also far away from the goings-on at the Sterling mansion.

The cottage hadn't been used for years, but the grounds keeper kept it clean and it was surprisingly cozy with the rain pattering on the roof. There was a lantern, a cot, a rolltop desk and boxes and tools that had been left there for storage. She found matches and lit the lantern, then sat on the cot and shivered in her wet dress.

Going out in the rain had not been the brightest thing she'd ever done. But at least it had taken her away from those awful women.

The simple fact was that she loved Cam. She would do anything for him. Even marry him, if it came to that.

"I'm sorry, Johnny," she whispered softly to the damp air. "But if he wants me, I will marry him."

Even if he only wants a part-time wife? her conscience nagged at her. Even if he only wants you to have his babies so he can go back to New York and get back to work?

"He didn't mean that," she said aloud. But even though the words hung in the air, she wasn't sure she believed them.

He hadn't deliberately hurt Johnny. That was certainly a relief, although it didn't excuse him from having ignored Johnny once he left him behind. Still, she could understand that. And he had certainly demonstrated remorse.

She could never have let herself really love anyone who had been cruel to Johnny. But she could understand someone who had hurt him without meaning to. Because she had done the same thing herself.

She heard footsteps outside, and she held her breath, knowing whoever it was would see the lantern light and probably stop in. If it were the grounds keeper...

The catch snapped open and there was Cam, an umbrella in one hand, a raincoat covering almost every other inch of him.

"I get it," he said, dropping the umbrella and shaking rain off the coat as he removed it. "It's a scavenger hunt, right? And my assignment is to go and bag the prettiest caterer in the Central Valley."

No matter what, no matter where, he could always make her smile. "Well, I guess you win," she said, playing along.

"Yahoo." He came toward her, eyes burning in the lantern light. "So what's my prize?"

She stared up at him, and he reached out with one hand and touched her wet hair.

"You're cold," he noted. "Here." He shrugged out of his dinner jacket and put it around her shoulders.

"You left the party," she said softly, still staring into his eyes.

"I left the party," he agreed. He sat down beside her on the cot. "I don't want any one of those women, Ann. You know that."

She nodded slowly. "I know that. What I don't know is who you do want."

A slight smile tugged at the corners of his wide mouth. "Don't lie to me, woman," he said huskily.

"You know very well who I want." His hand slipped under his jacket to cup her naked shoulder. "You know very well what I want," he said so softly she could barely hear the words.

And he was right. The answers to both those puzzles were candidly revealed in his blue eyes. She could read it all there. Could he see how much she loved him in return? If he didn't know by now, she would have to show him.

She closed her eyes, letting her head fall back as his mouth followed where his hand had led the way, and he began to kiss the tender skin near her collarbone, the silky expanse of her shoulder, moving across her as though he had to touch every part of her.

"Cam," she sighed, feeling the jacket fall away but not feeling any colder. He buried a hard, hot kiss at the base of her neck, his hands taking both her shoulders to hold her. Her skin was cool, slightly wet, and somehow the coolness over heat inflamed him. He wanted her with a driving urge that blotted out logic and thought and prudence. He wanted her with a clear, hungry desire that seemed to be all that mattered in the world. His hands held her in a hard, demanding embrace, and she responded, her body coming alive beneath his strength.

His fingers worked quickly, efficiently on the zipper at the back of her dress and then there was more flesh for his lips to explore and he found her breasts, the hard, tight nipples tantalizingly filling his mouth, the soft flesh molding to his touch.

She made a strangled sound and began to writhe beneath him. It had been so long since she'd felt herself open and come alive at a man's touch. She had forgotten how quickly she could be changed from a careful, thinking woman to a body that smoldered with need for a man.

"Hold on, Ann," he whispered, hardly knowing what he was saying. "Just wait for me."

She couldn't wait. He had to hurry. She reached to tug away his shirt, pushing at the fabric blindly, and he took care of the slacks. She needed him in a way that almost frightened her. It was as though that were all her body had been made for, all she needed to keep life itself in her veins. She had to have him. She had to have him now.

He came to her and she called out as he entered, clutching at him, her eyes wild with urgent need.

"Steady, Ann, take it easy," he murmured in her ear, but she couldn't stop, and he laughed with delight as his body took her into the storm, riding the tidal wave, peak after peak. He wanted to watch her, to enjoy her ecstasy, so he held back and waited until her shudders began to quiet, and her eyes could focus again.

"Hi," he said, his tongue playing with her ear. "Did you have a nice trip?"

She turned and looked at him, still shocked by what she'd experienced. "I . . . Cam . . . I . . ."

"Hush," he said, kissing her lips and beginning to trace their outline with his tongue. "It's my turn." He smiled down at her. "Want to come along?"

She had no choice. It didn't seem to be her body any longer. Some alien force had taken it over. Cam had but to tug on her nipple, or move inside her, and she was off again, riding the crest of the wave that never seemed to die down long enough for her to catch her breath.

He rode it, too, holding her so tightly she could never be afraid, whispering her name, warming her with his body. They were together, and that was the way it was meant to be. Maybe not forever, but at least for now.

They lay together on the tiny cot and touched as though they were just discovering bodies of the opposite sex, giggling softly, teasing, exploring. And then they made love again, softly, slowly, and with their eyes wide open.

It seemed like hours had gone by, perhaps even days. The rain was just a soft drizzle, hardly noticeable. And then a voice came crying through the trees and shattered their idyll.

"Cameron. Oh, yoo hoo, Cameron."

They froze in each other's arms.

Cam identified the voice first. "My God, it's Ursula."

"She's coming straight here. What'll we do?"

He rose and blew out the lantern, then slipped back on the cot beside Ann.

"Cameron. Are you in there?"

They lay very still and tried to think of some way to vanish into thin air as instantly as possible. This couldn't be happening. Everything had been so perfect. Maybe if they closed their eyes and wished her away...

She was jostling the catch on the door, and then, suddenly, like an answered prayer, a new voice filled the rainy night.

"Ursula. I've been looking all over for you."

Ann and Cam looked at one another and mouthed, in unison, "Bobby."

"What do you want?" Ursula asked impatiently. "I'm trying to find Cam."

Bobby came closer. They could hear his cowboy boots on the gravel.

"Well, you won't find him in there. Cam's gone, honey."

"Gone? What do you mean, gone?" Ursula cried in dismay.

"I mean the boy lit out. But I think I know a place where we could go to look for him."

"Take me there quickly. I want to catch him before he does something he might regret."

"Well, I'll tell you, Ursi, I don't think Cam's going to regret too much this evening." His voice, shimmering with humor, got slightly louder as he added, "But I do know the boy's going to owe me one."

"Whatever. Let's go, quickly."

"Sure, Ursula. My truck's parked right out by the gates. Let's go on into town, you and me." He laughed. "I've got a friend I want to reintroduce you to."

Their footsteps crunched on the wet ground and faded. Ann and Cam looked at each other, holding back their laughter until they dared to let it spill out.

"He's going to get her on that mechanical bull yet," she gasped.

"Just as long as he keeps her away from me, he can take her to Timbuktu for all I care."

"Oh, come on. Admit it. You kind of like Ursula. You certainly wouldn't want Bobby to hurt her."

He considered. "Not to hurt her, maybe. Just tease her a little."

"That is exactly what I think he has in mind." She sighed, lying back in Cam's arms.

Nine

Ann woke up in Cam's bed and smiled, stretching like a cat before a warm fire and snuggling deeper into the covers. He stretched beside her and she came to him, trying to let every inch of her naked body touch every inch of his.

"Were you dreaming?"

She nodded sleepily.

"Was I in it?"

"No, not really." She squinted, trying to remember it all. "I was dreaming I was on a long, white sailboat that was sailing across the water, and white birds were flying along with us. We were skimming along so very fast and my hair was blowing back. It almost felt as though I were flying, too."

"I'll tell you what your dream means," he informed her wisely. "You were you. The birds were your hopes and aspirations. And I—'' he grinned ''—I was the boat.''

''What?''

''Of course. Can't you see it? I was carrying you to paradise.''

''Oh brother.''

''Don't you know anything about symbolism in dreams?''

''I don't know much, but I know enough to know that's cockeyed.''

''No, really. I'm a very good dream interpreter.''

''I don't believe that for a minute. But I'll tell you what I do believe.'' She snuggled closer. ''I do believe you know how to make dreams come true.''

He laughed softly and cradled her in his arms. ''What's the best way you can think of to say good morning?'' he asked her softly.

She smiled. ''When in doubt, go with body language,'' she whispered back.

He laughed and they made slow, sweet love that she never wanted to end.

And then, Ursula was at the door.

''Cam?''

''Just be very quiet and she'll go away,'' he advised optimistically.

''Cameron, I know you're in there.'' There was a sound as though she had kicked the door. ''Never mind. Just come on down to the breakfast room within the hour, please. I want to say goodbye.''

They lay very still and listened to her footsteps going toward the stairway.

''Ursula is leaving,'' Cam said, almost sadly.

''I'll be leaving, too,'' Ann reminded him.

"Don't be ridiculous."

"You know I have to go, Cam. The party's over."
And she began to hum the tune that phrase brought to
mind.

"Right. Mock my misery if you will," he retorted,
kissing her soundly again and again. "You should be
more supportive. I need my friends behind me. I'm
going to have to face my mother soon."

She laughed. She knew it wasn't so much that he
was afraid of his mother, as it was that he was afraid
of hurting her. She liked that quality in him. As a
matter of fact, there wasn't a whole lot about him she
could complain about at the moment.

She slipped out of bed, taking the sheet along to
wrap around herself, and went to open the drapes,
flooding Cam with sunshine just as he had done to her
a few days ago.

"There you go. Rise and shine."

He groaned and dove back into the covers, and she
laughed. She started across the room, but something
caught her eye.

On the dresser was a stack of photographs. The one
on the top was a picture of Johnny.

"Cam, what are these?"

She stopped and began to go through the pictures.
There were eight or ten boys she remembered from
high school, including Cam. And Johnny.

"Oh." Cam sat up in the bed, suddenly wary.
"Those are some old pictures I found. I was going to
show them to you later."

"It's Johnny."

"Yeah, and a bunch of other guys from those days.
We all went down to go deep-sea fishing out of San

Diego one weekend. I took a camera along. Those are pictures we took on the boat.''

She looked through them again and again. Pictures of Johnny that she'd never seen before. It was as though she was seeing a whole side of him she'd never known about.

"Johnny," she whispered, touching his face in one picture. He would always be so young.

Cam watched her, his heart feeling like a heavy stone in his chest.

"I can't believe I've never seen these before."

In one he was holding up a very small fish and obviously trying to pretend it was a big one, playing for laughs. In another, he and Cam were arm in arm. In a third, he was holding hands with a little dark-eyed boy.

"Look at this," she said. "Look at the little boy, the look on his face."

"Yeah, I remember that. That was on the pier when we got back in. The kid was lost. Johnny must have spent a good hour looking for his parents. And then when he finally found them, the kid had gotten so attached to Johnny, he put his arms around Johnny's neck and wouldn't let go. We had to pry him off."

"He loved kids."

Tears were stinging in her eyes. "You know what the last thing was that he said to me?" she asked, her voice hoarse. "'I'm sorry I didn't give you a baby, Ann.' That was the very last thing he said."

Her voice choked on her last few words, and tears filled her eyes. Quickly, she looked away.

Cam turned and rammed his fist into his pillow.

God, this was impossible. He wanted to hate Johnny. He wanted to yell at Ann, to tell her to leave Johnny's ghost alone. For God's sake, it was over.

And yet, there was another side. There was all the harm he had done Johnny, all the casual lack of attention, things he could never make up now. How could he live with this torment? It just went on and on.

On one hand, he wanted to tear Johnny's memory to shreds and take his place in her heart. On the other, there was the guilt, the never-ending guilt.

He lay very still, listening to her go into the bathroom. There had to be some way to get Johnny out from between them. There had to be a way.

They met Mrs. Sterling in the hall outside the breakfast room.

"Mother, about last night..." Cam started, but she was shaking her head.

"You were better off out of it, dear," she told him sincerely. "When those women found out you had escaped, they set up such a howling, I was sure we'd be invaded by wolves. Not a one of them had any manners. They practically tore the place apart."

She sniffed, eyeing Ann. She'd seen the two of them come back in together, and she could put two and two in a column and add them right up. "I can see there will be no more parties, and perhaps that's better. We shall see, won't we?" She smiled at them both as though she had her own little secret, and she went into the kitchen.

They exchanged glances.

"One down, one to go," Cam muttered, as he held open the door for Ann and followed her into the breakfast room.

"I'm leaving, people." Ursula barely gave them time to sit down before she began. Dressed in a lovely suit with a tiny pillbox hat, she looked as though she belonged in the city, and certainly not out on a country estate like this.

"I have given up all hope of Cam coming to his senses and marrying me. My bags are packed. I'm ready to go."

"Ursula—"

"Wait. There's more. I called my mother early this morning and made her a proposition, which, luckily, she jumped at." She paused to emphasize the significance.

Cam smiled politely. "Are you going to tell us what this proposition is, or are we going to have to drag it out of you with tongs?"

Ursula moved back in her chair. She'd had experience with Cam. You never knew when he was only joking.

"No, I'll tell you," she said hurriedly. "I promised her a butler if she would give me the money I need to enlarge my restaurant. And she was desperate enough to agree to a fair exchange." She paused and smiled a bit nervously. "And so, I'm taking Maxwell with me."

"Taking Maxwell with you!" Ann and Cam both cried out the same thing at once.

"It's all right. Your mother okayed it. I know it's a terrible thing to do. But after all, you wouldn't give me a husband. So I'm taking your butler."

Ann and Cam glanced at each other and Cam said, "Just tell me one thing, Ursula. Did he agree to go?"

"Actually, he said he couldn't be happier."

Cam raised his eyebrows and shrugged almost imperceptibly. "If you two will excuse me, I have something I want to say to my mother."

He rose and left the room, and Ann looked speculatively at Ursula. "Did you . . . have a good time last night?" she asked, watching for the reaction.

"Last night?" Ursula looked at her suspiciously. "What do you know about last night?"

"Oh . . . nothing at all."

"If you mean, did he get me on that stupid contraption they call a mechanical bull, the answer is, no way. I was in luck. The thing broke down."

"Oh." Ann hid her smile. "Well, we're going to miss you, Ursula."

She heaved a heavy sigh. "Believe it or not, I'm going to miss you all, too."

She started for the front door and Ann followed her.

"What about . . . Bobby?" Ann asked, probing.

"Bobby? He's a peasant. A Neanderthal."

Ann waited, noting the frown between Ursula's brows. She was still thinking about the subject.

Ursula stopped just before she reached the door, and turned, slowly. "He's a rough, elemental sort, don't you think?" Her eyes were slightly glazed. "Quite basic in his needs and . . ." She remembered where she was and shook herself. "Oh. Well, I've called a cab, and I'm ready to go." She reached for the doorknob. "Goodbye to you all. I wish you well, in spite of everything."

She flung open the door, and there, leaning against the frame in a most insolent manner, was Bobby.

"I sent away your cab," he drawled, smiling at Ursula. "My truck is here and ready to go. I'll drive you."

Ursula looked at Ann for help and found none. "But . . . but Maxwell . . ."

"Is already sitting in the back seat. He'll make a great chaperon." He made a flourishing gesture toward the vehicle. "I'm ready to drive you all the way to Sausalito, honey. Just hop in."

"Well . . ." Ursula looked wary but game. "I guess that might be all right." She started down the driveway.

Bobby saluted Ann. "See you later," he said with a grin. "We're off." He turned back just before he got into the truck. "We're just making one little stop at Duke's Country Swing. Gotta see a man about a bull. Seems they got it fixed early this morning. Yippee!"

There was a shriek from Ursula, but it was lost in the roar of the engine, and soon all that was left was a trail of dust.

Ann sighed and shook her head, and Cam came up beside her, slipping an arm around her shoulders.

"She's gone."

"But not forgotten." Cam laughed softly. "Here's the story. My venerable mother had had enough of Maxwell's sour face, and she was more than happy to give him his walking papers." He grinned. "So we're butlerless, but contented."

Her smile was bittersweet. "I'd better pack."

"No." He took her hands in his own and gazed down at her. "Not today. Give me one full day, Ann.

We'll spend it together, and we won't think of anything but our own selfish happiness. Okay?''

Something that had been very tight inside her uncoiled. "That would be wonderful," she told him, smiling happily. "What shall we do?"

"Take a picnic lunch down by the river. Pick daisies. Walk for miles through the meadows. Play tennis. Make love. Go dancing. Stroll under the moon." His arms slid around her. "Whatever you want, Ann. I'm at your command."

She reached up and touched his cheek with the palm of her hand. "Let's go," she said urgently. "Right now. Let's leave everything and everyone behind, and just go."

He read the anxiety in her eyes but he refused to acknowledge it. They would banish all worries today. They would live for each other and never look back. If only it would work.

They had a beautiful day, and another wonderful night, and then it was time for Ann to clear up her operation and head for home.

She had a long talk with Mrs. Sterling, who was being quite philosophical about how her plans had fallen through. They parted on good terms. Mrs. Sterling even gave her a hug. She packed her books and pans and cooking gadgets and Cam drove her back to her little house.

The ranunculuses were finished and so were the Iceland poppies, but the marigolds and cosmos were in full bloom, and tomatoes were setting on the vines. Her house looked neat and trim and welcoming. It should have been good to be home. But somehow, it wasn't quite what she'd expected.

Cam helped her carry her things in. The mood between them had suddenly become strained and the silences were heavy. Ann went around opening windows as if that would bring in lighter air and return them to their carefree mood of yesterday.

Cam watched her, realizing what she was doing. It was this damn place. It was too full of Johnny. Johnny was everywhere you looked. His things. His pictures. His house. His girl.

He went to the bedroom and looked in, immediately noticing that she had changed the picture by the bed. There was a dark, frustrated rage building inside him. This wasn't right. It couldn't be happening. He refused to be cut out by a dead man.

"Cam."

She came to him. She knew it, too. It had haunted them yesterday, for all the happiness they had shared.

He reached for her and took her into his arms, lowering his head to take her parted lips, his mouth hard and questioning, trying to find an answer, trying to blot out the darkness that seemed to lurk at the edges of their space. Her tongue met his and danced with it, stroking, searching, reaching for a tender connection that would serve to express how much she cared.

Her hands slid under his shirt, making a hot trail up the lean, smooth muscles of his hard chest, her fingers flexing against his skin. He groaned, his mouth against her mouth, and his hands took her hips and pulled them into his, beginning the rhythm of thrust and surge that would take them where the both wanted to go.

She moved against him with a fever that told him she wanted to blot it out, too. That gave him hope. He tore at her clothes, needing her quickly, and she cried out, reaching for him, touching, stroking, urging his readiness just as his hands were urging hers.

He wanted her there, on her bed, in front of the pictures. That was the way it had to be, and she understood. She lay with him and in a certain way, she felt freer than she ever had at his house, freer to say his name aloud, freer to call for him to hurry, to let her voice rise and cry her need for him.

They came together and it was right and high and hard, a soaring that touched the sky and wrote ecstasy upon it.

Lying back, they tried to catch their breath. Cam felt a sweep of triumph. They had made it. For just a moment, they had banished the fear and found perfection.

But the moment passed. As they lay together, still breathing as though they had run a mile, perfection slid away and left them with reality. And reality meant that ghosts were part of everything they did.

They took a shower together and played and laughed and talked for another hour, while they shared a lunch, but they both knew it was only a holding action. They had tried, and they had ultimately failed. What they didn't know, and didn't even dare talk about, was what they were going to do about it.

Finally Cam couldn't take it any longer. They were sitting together on her porch steps, watching a neighborhood cat fight off blue jays, and waiting for the sunset to fill the sky with color.

"This isn't working, is it?" he asked bluntly.

She turned toward him, her eyes huge and frightened. "Don't say that," she said.

"You know it as well as I do. It's not coming together the way it should."

"We need time. It'll work itself out."

He was shaking his head. "No. Time isn't what we need. If anything, we've had too much time." His face was darkened with pain. "Maybe if I'd stayed that night of the senior picnic after I kissed you...maybe if I'd kissed you again, and we'd faced Johnny with how we felt right then..."

She was trembling. How did he know she'd loved him even then? Had he felt it that night? Had it always been with him, just as it had always been with her?

"Johnny told me to take care of his girl, and instead, I stole her."

"Cam, don't do this," she whispered, letting her black hair hide most of her face.

"And then I walked away. Who knows? Maybe that's one of the reasons I didn't look back. Because I knew what I had done."

"Cam..." She reached out and took his hand in hers, pressing it to her heart. "Don't do this to yourself."

But he went on as though she hadn't spoken. "We have to live with the consequences of that. It's all around us. We can't escape it."

"What does that mean?"

He looked up again, his eyes shaded with agony. "I don't know. Maybe it means we were destined to want each other but not to have each other."

"Cam!"

He drew her into his arms, holding her tenderly. "I can't bear this. This is torture—to have you, and yet not to have you." His arm tightened and his voice became rough. "I need all of you, Ann. I can't stand just having a part."

He looked down into her face. "You can't even promise me that you can ever give me all, can you?"

"Oh, Cam, I wish I could. I think with time . . ."

"No." He kissed her, tasting of salt and regret. "I want you, Ann. But I can't have you. He's always there between us. I can't live this way. Every time I look at you, I see him somewhere in the shadows of your eyes."

Slowly, gently, he disentangled himself from her arms and rose.

"Goodbye, Ann, I'm going back to New York. It's time to get back into the life I've known for so long. Let me know if you think of a way to get Johnny out from between us."

And he walked to his car, got in and drove away.

Ten

___

Ann cried all that night and wandered around the next day like a zombie. At first she was angry with him for giving up so easily. But eventually she began to admit to herself that he was right. Johnny was still a part of her, and she couldn't find a way to release him.

She cried herself to sleep the next night, but she slept well, and when she got up that morning, she looked into the mirror and put on a fresh face.

Crying had taken up too much of her past. There would be no more tears. She had mourned too long for Johnny. She wasn't going to make the same mistake about Cam.

She got busy right away, setting up her supplies and calling contacts to let people know she was back in business. The response she got overwhelmed her.

"Hey, no kidding? You're back?" was the typical comment. "I hear you did a fantastic job with the Sterling parties. There was an article in the paper about you. Did you see it? Listen, I've got a list of people who have been asking about you, and now that you're free to take on other work, I'm sure we've got enough here to keep you busy for a month."

At first she was a little puzzled. She'd never had a problem finding work, but there had never been a stampede to her door. Now, everybody seemed to want her. Even people who had never thought of having their affairs catered before were calling and asking for quotes. Before the week was out, she was calling friends to ask if anyone knew of any teenagers who would like to work with her for the rest of the summer. She had enough bookings to carry her right into the fall season.

It was nice but a bit hectic. And then, to make matters worse, everyone in town suddenly seemed to find other things they needed her for. The community center called and asked her to speak to their cooking class. The local supermarket wanted to know if she could put together a demonstration for their Saturday specials. The high school called and asked her to volunteer time for the summer school career week. And twenty-two teenagers came by, applying for the two openings she had.

"You're famous," Jenny Wilson, her best friend since elementary school told her when she complained. "Everywhere I go, people are talking about you."

"Famous? But why? I haven't done anything special."

"It's the Sterling connection, of course. You link up with them, you're asking for it. Everything the Sterlings do has always been big news around here."

"I know, but all I did was work for them."

"Putting on parties that were the talk of the valley. You're in the big leagues now, Ann. I wouldn't be surprised if a magazine didn't call and ask for an interview."

It was sort of fun at first, but it quickly developed into a real pain. She couldn't run down to the corner convenience store at six in the morning and grab doughnuts and the morning paper anonymously as she had always done in the past. Now she invariably ran into someone who knew who she was and wanted to talk about it. When she was jogging, people slowed their cars alongside and tried to strike up conversations. Men she'd never seen before tried to ask her out. Children pointed at her on the street.

"Pretty soon, dogs will begin howling when they hear my name mentioned," she grumbled to Jenny. "They'll name the toxic dump after me, and the TV stations will call me in as an expert witness the next time someone dies of botulism."

"The price of fame," Jenny told her with a grin. "At least you're making lots of money."

That she was, hand over fist. People were actually getting into bidding wars for her services. She had one man call and cancel a date for the Jordans, only to call back later, disguising his voice, and try to book the same night for a party named Curtis. When she called the Jordans to check, she found out they had never canceled at all. The Curtis person was just trying to steal their appointment.

So here she was, earning more and enjoying it less.

In some small way, she began to realize this was a bit like what Cam had gone through ten years before. She could understand better than she ever had before how he might grow cynical and learn to distrust people. She found herself closing off from people, unwilling to give them a chance for fear they only wanted something from her. It wasn't a pleasant way to live, but she managed.

And she missed Cam.

She tried to pretend otherwise. She managed to block out everything but a dull ache for most of the day. But come nighttime, she was a basket case.

Even if she succeeded in holding memories at bay while she was awake, they came on full force in her dreams. She dreamed of his touch, his kiss, his handsome face, and usually awoke clutching her pillow as though she could shake it hard and produce the man she loved.

But he was never really there. And she would have to shake off the melancholy of that reality before she could jump-start her day and get on with it.

She took a trip to San Francisco and bought herself a new wardrobe to go with her new position as catering superstar—lots of classy suits like Ursula wore. Wearing them made her feel like a whole new person, and when she got home, she decided her house needed an overhaul, too.

Out with the old, in with the new.

She ordered new drapes, bought a new set of living room furniture, installed new carpets. And when the time came to rearrange all her knickknacks, she found herself setting everything of Johnny's aside.

It came as quite a shock when she realized what she was doing. She stood and stared at the pile. There was Johnny's baseball that she had always left on the bookcase shelf. His All-League certificate had always hung on the wall near the kitchen. His favorite little sculpture of a boy and his dog—when you came right down to it, she had always hated that thing. And then there were all his pictures.

Her heart was beating very fast and she forced herself to look at what she was doing. Why hadn't she done this years ago? She had thought three years ago when she had taken off her rings that she was signaling to herself and the world that she was casting off widow's weeds. But she didn't really follow through. It was high time she did.

She gathered all of Johnny's things into a box and carried it to the attic. After putting it down in an empty spot, she stood back and looked at the contents. Strangely, there were no tears today.

"Johnny," she said softly. "I loved you long and well. I could never love you as fully as you deserved, but I did the best I could. And now it's time to say goodbye."

She went downstairs and waited for the guilt, waited for the feeling of dread to develop in her chest. But nothing happened. It was true. She was finally free.

Free to live her life. Free to do anything she wanted to do.

And what she wanted to do was to go to Cam. How could she have waited so long?

She had three long days before her next party, and things were running smoothly. She could leave the final preparations to her new assistants. Excitement filled her as she dialed the airline and made a reservation on the next flight out to New York.

She was halfway across the country before the doubts began to kick in. It had been over a month since she'd seen him. A lot could happen in that amount of time. Would he want to see her? Perhaps he had found someone new by now. What if she walked in and saw that look on his face that said, "Uh-oh. What's she doing here?"

That would kill her. Absolutely kill her.

She got off the airplane at Kennedy and stood there for a few minutes, contemplating finding the next flight back home and then talking to him by phone instead of in person. But slowly, her chin rose. What was she, a woman or a wimp? She'd come all this way to say something to Cam, and by George, she was going to say it.

She'd worn one of her new suits and she knew she looked good. That helped give her confidence. She took a cab into Manhattan and went directly to the Sterling Building and the executive floor.

"Can you direct me to Mr. Cameron Sterling's office?" she asked the receptionist.

"Right that way." The woman indicated tall, double doors. "But I think he's in a meeting right now. You'd better talk to his secretary."

Ann started toward the door, but on the way she noticed a group of men behind a glass wall. She stopped to look more closely, and there was Cam.

Her heart skipped a beat and she gasped, trying hard to hold it all together. There he was, every beautiful inch of him, in deep conversation and not at all aware she was nearby. She stared for a long time, unable to tear her gaze away. He was so gorgeous. Would he be glad to see her?

She turned back toward his office and there was his secretary, leaning over a partition to talk to someone in another section. Taking advantage of the opportunity, Ann slipped into his office and closed the door without being seen.

That was when panic set in. Here she was in New York, taking it for granted he would want to see her. She should have called first.

Pacing nervously around the office, she looked at his books, his netsuke collection, his Remington. The office was richly appointed. The carpet was so thick, she felt as though she could swim in it. The desk was a huge oak affair that took up a third of the room.

She walked over to look at it more carefully, and something on the desktop caught her eye. It was a letter. And the handwriting was Johnny's. She would have known it anywhere.

She stood for a moment, blinking, and then she reached for the letter and began to read it.

Hey, Cam, remember me? How've you been? Ann is making me write this letter, and even though I always say Ann knows best, this time I know she's wrong.

I'm running my father's store now, and it's about to go under. Ann seems to think that a nice fat loan from you would save it. I know better. The days of the corner grocery are about over. There's a big new supermarket just a block away. The day they dedicated that building was the day the bell started to toll for our place. But that's progress. Things change.

You're a big wheel in the big city. Ya done good, boy. We're proud of you. But I know people like you don't answer their own mail. Some secretary will see this letter and file it away. You probably won't ever see it. Still, I decided it would be good to write to you, while I still have time.

I'm checking out, Cam. I've been diagnosed and I've only got a few weeks to go. I haven't told Ann yet. I'm trying to find a way to tell her.

She's a wonderful woman. She's strong. She doesn't really need me, and we don't have any kids. But I sure would feel better if I knew she would marry someone who appreciates her after I'm gone. She'll make some man a great wife, and some kids a great mother.

I want to thank you for the kind of friend you were to me that year in high school. I wish we had kept in touch better, but I know how it is. After school, you drift apart. But that year meant a lot. Knowing you changed me, Cam. I'm grateful.

Forget the money. It won't do me any good. But the one thing you could do for me is this—the next time you come home for a visit, look up Ann and see how she's doing. That's all I really want from you, Cam.

You take care, Cam.

All the best, Johnny

It was just like Johnny to write such a letter. She laughed softly. She should have insisted he show it to her before he sent it. The rat! What a backhanded way to ask for a loan. And the request to have Cam look in on her—had Johnny known? Had he sensed the feelings she had for Cam? She would never know. And when you came right down to it, it hardly mattered anymore.

She waited, but the sick feeling didn't come. She was warmed by this letter, touched by it. But that other thing that had held her in thrall all these years, that was truly gone.

There were voices outside the door. Cam was back from his meeting. She turned, heart in her throat, and then he was in the room.

She stared at him, trying to read his thoughts in his face, but he kept it blank and watched her.

She held out the letter. "Where did you find this?"

His eyes shifted to the letter and back again. "I've been spending my evenings going through the old files in a warehouse near the waterfront. I found that last night. I've been trying to call you all day."

"I was on a flight, coming here."

He nodded. "You read it?" he asked warily, searching her eyes. He couldn't tell how she was taking it. Would this trigger another wave of guilt? Would knowing Johnny had suspected there was something, little as it was, between them all along make her turn away from him?

"Yes. I read it." She put it down and drew her arms around herself, wondering why he was making no effort to come close. "I . . . Johnny was such a love, wasn't he?"

Cam's heart sank. "Yes," he replied woodenly. "He was a great friend and a wonderful husband."

But he's dead, he wanted to add. He's dead and we have to put him where he belongs.

She lifted her face and met his eyes, gazing at him wonderingly. "I loved Johnny," she said clearly. "But Johnny is gone. And Cam..." She stumbled on his name, so frightened of what she was about to do. "I...I love you, now. I love you so much, I can hardly bear to be without you." His image was swimming before her because tears were filling her eyes. She reached toward him ineffectually.

"If you can't love me back...if you can't stand what Johnny was to me once, tell me now. Because I have to know, I have to learn to harden myself...."

"Ann." He said her name like a prayer, and then his arms were around her and her face was pressed to his chest. "Ann, I've been going crazy here without you. I can't keep my mind on my work. All I've been doing is searching for that letter, because I had this weird idea in my head that somehow that letter was going to make everything right between us."

"No," she said, her voice trembling slightly. "The letter doesn't make it right. Only we can do that." She looked up into his face. "I think I can do it, Cam. But do you?"

His kiss stopped her words. "I love you, Ann," he said huskily, his arms holding her tighter and tighter. "Oh God, I love you so much. I have to have you with me, no matter what, even if that means I have to take Johnny, too."

"No." She was shaking her head, her hair flying about them both. "No, I've conquered that problem. I really have. I don't love anyone but you, Cam. And I never will."

They stood there in each other's arms for a long, long time, murmuring softly, kissing, holding on to the new happiness they still weren't completely secure with. Security would come with time and experience. It was within their grasp.

"Have you eaten?" he asked at last, lovingly brushing stray hair away from her cheek and letting his gaze take in every curve, every angle of her, as though he needed to fill his senses with everything about her, having been deprived for so long. "Would you like to go out?"

She shook her head, smiling, happy as she hadn't been in years. "I just want you to hold me, for hours and hours."

His old grin returned. "That can be arranged." He drew away from her and went to the intercom on his desk. "Tiffany, please hold all my calls. I'm taking a long, long meeting, and I don't want to be disturbed. Not for anything at all."

Striding briskly to the door, he locked it and turned back to her, gesturing toward the huge, comfortable couch. "We've got all day," he said as he drew her down into his arms. "And all night, too."

"I have to go back day after tomorrow," she said with regret. "I've got a party to do."

"Good," he said. "I'll go with you."

"Really?" She searched his blue eyes. "And then what?"

"I'll stay." He kissed her temple, using his lips to find the pulse there. "I'm wrapping up things here as it is. I'm sick of this life with its stress and frantic pace." His long, strong fingers began unbuttoning the silk-covered buttons of her blouse. "I want to go home and relax." He dropped a row of warm kisses down her neck. "Take life easy...." His hand slipped in under the straps on her shoulder, shoving them gently aside. "Maybe start a small business..." He looked at her naked shoulder, his eyes narrowing. "Get married..." He pressed his lips to the hollow below her collarbone. "Have kids."

She laughed low in her throat, her fingers sinking into his thick hair and tugging. "You don't ask much, do you?"

"Ann, my darling, I've told you before. I want it all." He gazed up at her, the question alive in his eyes. "Tell me, lady. Are you in a marrying mood?"

* * * * *

BEGINNING IN FEBRUARY FROM

SILHOUETTE®

Desire™

Western Lovers

An exciting new series by Elizabeth Lowell
Three fabulous love stories
Three sexy, tough, tantalizing heroes

In February,	*Man of the Month* Tennessee Blackthorne in *OUTLAW*
In March,	Cash McQueen in *GRANITE MAN*
In April,	Nevada Blackthorne in *WARRIOR*

WESTERN LOVERS—Men as tough and untamed as
the land they call home.

Only in *Silhouette Desire*!

Silhouette Special Edition

proudly presents
the long-awaited "prequel" volume of

LOVE AND GLORY
by
LINDSAY McKENNA
Dawn of Valor

In the summer of '89, Silhouette Special Edition premiered three novels celebrating America's men and women in uniform: LOVE AND GLORY, by bestselling author Lindsay McKenna. Featured were the proud Trayherns, a military family as bold and patriotic as the American flag—three siblings valiantly battling the threat of dishonor, determined to triumph . . . in love and glory.

Now, discover the roots of the Trayhern brand of courage, as parents Chase and Rachel relive their earliest heartstopping experiences of survival and indomitable love, in

Dawn of Valor, Silhouette Special Edition #649

This month, experience the thrill of LOVE AND GLORY—from the very beginning!

Available at your favorite retail outlet, or order your copy by sending your name, address, zip or postal code, along with a check or money order (please do not send cash) for $2.95, plus 75¢ postage and handling, payable to Silhouette Reader Service to:

In the U.S.
3010 Walden Ave.
P.O. Box 1396
Buffalo, NY 14269-1396

In Canada
P.O. Box 609
Fort Erie, Ontario
L2A 5X3

Please specify book title with your order. Canadian residents add applicable federal and provincial taxes.

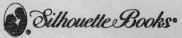

Silhouette Books

DV-1A